Now Naaman,
commander of the
army of the king of
Syria, was a great and
honorable man in the eyes of his
master, because by him the LORD had
given victory to Syria. He was also a
mighty man of valor, but a leper. And
the Syrians had gone out on raids, and
had brought back captive a young girl
from the land of Israel. She waited on
Naaman's wife. Then she said to her
mistress, "If only my master were
with the prophet who is in Samaria!
For he would heal him of his leprosy."

*And Naaman went in and told his master,*
*saying, "Thus and thus said the girl who is*
*from the land of Israel."*
*Then the king of Syria said, "Go now, and*
*I will send a letter to the king of Israel."*

—2 KINGS 5:1–5 (NKJV)

*Ordinary Women* of the BIBLE
✦

*Ordinary Women* of the BIBLE

# THE PROPHET'S SONGBIRD
## ATARAH'S STORY

ROSEANNA M. WHITE

*Ordinary Women* of the BIBLE

✦

# THE PROPHET'S SONGBIRD

## ATARAH'S STORY

## Dedication

To Rachel, one of many amazing songbirds in my life.
Couldn't do it without you!

# Cast of
# CHARACTERS

**Biblical**

**Ben-Hadad II** • also known as Hadadezer, king of Aram-Damascus (Syria)

**Elisha** • the prophet in Israel

**Gehazi** • Elisha's servant and aide

**Joram** • the king of Israel

**Naaman** • a Syrian general in Ben-Hadad's army

**Fictional**

**Abner** • a student at the School of the Sons of the Prophets

**Atarah** • daughter of Johash and his wife

**Dafna** • head cook in Naaman's house, a Hebrew

**Izla** • Lebario's wife, Ram's mother, Ramina's aunt

**Johash** • one of the prophets under Elisha who served as a teacher at the School of the Sons of the Prophets

**Lebario** • Ram's father, political adversary of Naaman, uncle of Ramina

**Lilya** • daughter (second child) of Naaman and Ramina

**Malak** • son (first child) of Naaman and Ramina

**Ram** • soldier and political adversary of Naaman, cousin of Ramina

**Ramina** • the wife of Naaman

**Seena** • head guard of Naaman's house, trainer

**Tavi** • a student at the School of the Sons of the Prophets

O God, my heart is steadfast;
I will sing and give praise, even with my glory.
Awake, lute and harp!
I will awaken the dawn.
I will praise You, O LORD, among the peoples,
And I will sing praises to You among the nations.
For Your mercy is great above the heavens,
And Your truth reaches to the clouds.

Psalm 108:1–4 (NKJV)

# CHAPTER ONE

The prophet was coming, and the thrill of it made notes of joy burst in Atarah's mind and spill from her lips in a hum. She pulled the last round of bread from the side of the oven and offered it to her mother with a grin. Tonight, perhaps, Elisha himself would dine with them. Or tomorrow. Soon he would arrive, and the entire School of the Sons of the Prophets would feast together to welcome him.

"Thank you, Atarah." Imma took the bread and slid it onto the table, huffing a breath when the twins darted by, nearly knocking her from her feet. "Channah! Havah! Sit and eat."

Her little sisters jostled each other for their favorite spot, ignoring their mother's chiding. Atarah pressed her lips against another grin. Barely five, those two could try the patience of anyone. Imma might be capable of making the hardest of hearts crack in grief when she lifted her voice in mourning, but inspiring the twins to behave themselves was another talent altogether—one only Abba seemed able to master.

Fortunate, then, that he strolled in now, silencing the twins with one well-aimed glare before sending a wink Atarah's way. "Something smells delicious." He settled against his usual cushion and smiled at them all. He should have been out already, helping the other prophets care for the animals, teaching his students how to listen for Yahweh in every stirring of the breeze, every bleat of a lamb, every buzz of a bee. *"Our God is a living God,"* she'd heard him saying to Tavi last week, *"so we seek Him through the tending of life. We see the sacred in the miracle of this world He has created."*

Tavi—a student at the School of the Sons of the Prophets only for the past three years, but unquestionably Abba's favorite—had nodded in that solemn way of his.

Channah snuggled against Atarah's side the moment she folded her legs and sat. She turned her sweet little face up to her too. "What song are you going to sing when the prophet arrives, Atarah?"

Her stomach danced a bit at the question. It was Elisha himself who had first invited her to sing a psalm of praise before the school, when she was scarcely older than Channah and Havah were now. But it still made her anxious to do so when he was here—anxious and eager both. It was Yahweh she wanted to praise and please with her voice, ultimately, but... but one could not get much closer to Him than His prophet.

"The one hundred forty-fifth, I think." It was the first song she had ever sung in front of the school. *I will extol You, my God, O King; and I will bless Your name forever and ever.*

Havah grinned over at her. "What about this morning? Will you sing the one about Him training my hands for war?" Havah pulled her arm back, as if she held a miniature bow.

Abba gusted out a sigh. "Havah. Leave the warring to your brothers."

Havah's brows drew together like a thundercloud. And the storm was only cut off because two of those brothers chose that moment to hurry into the room, all elbows and knees as they jostled each other into place.

Atarah grinned at the boys—eight and ten now—and tried not to miss the eldest of them too much. Joshua had been away from home for two years now as he studied to be a scribe, but she had yet to get used to his absence.

Imma turned to the table with the last of the breakfast dishes in her hands, sending a weary look toward the twins. "Perhaps Atarah should sing a plea for relief from persecutors today."

She chuckled and then let the conversation drop while Abba led them in a short prayer of thanksgiving. But while talk afterward turned to the weather and when Elisha might arrive, Atarah let the many songs she knew float through her mind. Which one today? Something joyful, because the prophet was coming. Something happy, because the Lord had blessed the school so richly. Something...something that had a hope of teasing a rare smile to Tavi's lips.

"What do you think, Atarah?"

"Hmm?" She looked up at her father. His plate was empty. Even more surprising, so was hers.

His smile was as soft and warm as the bread she could scarcely remember eating. "I was only saying it will be a joy to see Gehazi again. And that perhaps you could plan to sing his favorite song after the meal too."

"Of course." She reached for his empty plate, stacked it with hers, and then raised a questioning brow toward the twins, neither of whom had finished their yogurt yet. They stopped their giggling long enough to scoop some onto an apple slice and stuff it into their mouths.

Abba's hand landed on her shoulder. "Whenever they arrive—be it tonight or tomorrow—we will have another announcement too. Something I think you will be most pleased to celebrate."

The last time her father had worn that particular expression, it had been when he informed the family that arrangements had been made for Joshua to be educated as a scribe—a true honor, and one that had made her elder brother beam with joy. *She* had not been quite so happy to say farewell to him, though she was of course bursting with pride.

Was this news that he had completed his studies and would be coming home? Or perhaps that final arrangements had been made for his marriage? Atarah would certainly be thrilled when Joshua returned and wed Sahar—then she would finally get to claim her friend as her sister.

The younger children were bustling away from the table with their usual noise, so she asked for no clarification now. She simply smiled and nodded, noting that the light in Abba's eyes was the simple kind. Not the one that shone from them on those occasions when the Spirit of God came upon him and he spoke something divine. This was not Johash son of Ner, one of the prophets, who spoke—just Abba.

"Hurry, Atarah!" Channah shouted from the doorway. "I see Tavi and Abner coming!"

It was all the inspiration Atarah needed to rush the plates to the bench and fly back to the sleeping chamber the girls all shared for her head covering. They would scour the breakfast dishes later, after the school had joined together for prayers and song and then dismissed the students to their classes and tasks.

She joined her sisters outside just as the two young men reached their house. Abner lifted a hand, smiling. "Good morning! How are the loveliest ladies in Ramah today?"

He never missed an opportunity to smile at her, nor to compliment her or Imma. He was without question the handsomest student at the school and the most charming, and he was of an age to choose a wife and start a household of his own. All the girls in the region had been vying for his attention, trying to convince their fathers to enter negotiations with his.

Imma, a step behind her, greeted him while Atarah tucked a strand of hair under her headscarf. She barely kept a frown from her brows. She had always found him handsome too, of course. It was a simple fact. And a few years ago, she had entertained dreams about becoming his wife someday. It had seemed likely. Their fathers were friends, both teachers at the school, their families equals.

Now, though, the thought made no notes of anticipation trill through her mind, no song spring to her lips. Abner was a friend. But she had no particular yearning to be his wife.

That was not the news Abba would have for her...was it?

Her gaze darted past him, to Tavi. Two inches shorter, not quite as handsome if one were judging a face by symmetry and whatever else made one person more beautiful than another. Never did he greet anyone with a carefree smile.

But his hands were already caught, one in each of the twins', and he was listening to their chatter with rapt attention, nodding along to whatever they were saying as they tugged him toward the central courtyard of the compound.

She could still see him as he had been when first the prophet brought him here, three years ago. Lanky and thin, yes, but worse than that. He had been hollow. A pottery shell surrounding a void. As if all his heart, all his spirit had drained from him when he watched the Syrians slaughter his family in a raid.

Elisha had seen something in him though. He had brought him here and whispered a few words to her parents. Abba had taken the young man under his wing, and Imma had made it a point to sing whenever he was near.

Never would Atarah forget the soul-deep weeping she had heard one evening, as finally that void filled—with grief. Finally, six months after their deaths, Imma's songs inspired him to let himself mourn his parents.

After that, the healing could begin. Atarah had made it her personal challenge to follow up Imma's work on his heart by inspiring him to smile again. More often than not, she failed to win an *actual* smile...but she had become a master at making his eyes twinkle with otherwise hidden mirth.

She would sing his favorite this morning. The ninety-second Psalm.

*O Lord, how great are Your works!*
*Your thoughts are very deep.*

*A senseless man does not know,*
*Nor does a fool understand this.*
*When the wicked spring up like grass,*
*And when all the workers of iniquity flourish,*
*It is that they may be destroyed forever.*

He looked over his shoulder as they entered the courtyard, his gaze snagging on hers for a split second. He had
strange eyes—a bluish green, so striking against the tone of
his skin and his dark hair. The other girls, when they were
not dreaming of a betrothal with Abner, were swooning over
those eyes.

He gave her no smile, of course. But oh, the twinkle. Atarah
grinned back at him and followed her father toward the dais
from which he would speak the morning prayer.

The students were a bit rowdy this morning, their voices a
babble of excited speculation as she took her position beside
Abba. Everyone was anticipating the prophet's arrival as much
as her own family was. She chuckled and leaned close to her
father. "Good luck teaching them the Law today."

He breathed a laugh of his own. "I think perhaps it would
be a good day to work on the new storehouse instead." He nodded toward the half-finished structure on the outskirts of their
compound.

Yahweh Yireh had blessed them indeed this year—their
crops had produced a bounty beyond any Atarah could remember, and the animals had been particularly fruitful too. They
would have enough not only to get through the winter and

spring before the next harvest, but to supply the needs of anyone in the community who lacked.

Abba lifted a hand, but silence did not reign. He shouted, but no one seemed to hear. So he turned to her with a roll of his eyes and an indulgent smile. "Daughter."

She grinned and stepped forward. Closed her eyes. Let the wind singing through the branches of the sycamores instill their melody in her spirit. And she sang.

As always, she began with a familiar melody, the one traditionally paired with the lyrics of the song. But rarely could she leave it at that. New notes always sprang into her mind, and she had learned long ago to let them.

Within moments, the crowd had hushed. Here and there, another voice would join in—the deep harmony of Abner's father's bass, the sweet soprano of the youngest students. They sang the traditional melodies, leaving her to run up a scale or give her notes wings like a bird.

Her heart pounded in her chest as the last lines spilled from her lips. This was living. This was praising. This was communing with El Roi, the God who saw her. She opened her eyes again, looking at the crowd not to see what they thought, but seeking one face.

*There.* Tavi stood at the back, as usual, hands still lifted toward heaven. They lowered as he opened his own eyes again. Looked her way.

Would he smile? Would he grant her that gift today? Maybe. Yes! There, the corners of his mouth lifted, the light in his eyes reached her even from here. The—

A shout pierced the morning calm, and then what sounded like a thousand more, from all around the low walls of the compound. It was a sound she had never heard before but one that made terror dig claws into her spine.

They were under attack.

# CHAPTER TWO

A n attack! To safety!" Abba shouted the warning, but still
she could barely hear it over the din. Dark-clad figures
were vaulting over the walls in some places, pushing them
down in others, chariots thundering in, horses snorting. Men
flooded the compound with weapons raised that caught the
sun's fire and seemed to shoot it straight at her eyes. Swords.
Arrows. Spears.

Her father's fingers dug into her shoulder. "Get the
children. Take them to the cellar. Hurry!"

She could only nod and obey, her thoughts too jumbled to
come up with any plan of their own. The children—that was
all that mattered. The boys, the twins. She searched for them
in the melee, searched for Imma, who would be about the same
task, she knew.

There—her mother had one of the twins by the hand, but
where was the other? And the boys—Tavi had them, one on his
hip and the other's hand in his.

Havah, though. Where was Havah?

People darted this way and that, those old enough no
doubt running for weapons, the younger ones running for
shelter. Screams, shouts everywhere. Had the situation not
been so real, she would have covered her ears to protect them

from the angry clashes of metal on metal, the guttural cries, the utter cacophony.

She had no such leisure. She paused in her mad dash just long enough to search the surging crowd again for some sign of her youngest sister. Though when she spotted her, slung over the shoulder of a stranger in terrible armor, it was no relief.

"No! Havah!"

With every ounce of speed the Lord granted her, she darted for the raider and her daring, beautiful little sister who was screaming for all she was worth, pounding the soldier's back and kicking like a wild thing. *That is right, Havah! Fight him! Get him to put you down!*

A building had been set ablaze up ahead. Never would Atarah have called such a thing a blessing, except that the kidnapper looked toward it just as Atarah was drawing near. It was perhaps the only moment she would have to catch him off guard.

She took it. Arms wide, she sprang, flew, praying Yahweh Nissi would give her wings to save her sister. A scream tore from her throat—a battle cry. She collided with the soldier's back, her arms closing around his throat.

His grip on Havah must have loosened, praise be to the Lord. Her sister dropped to the ground, her own battle cry joining Atarah's as she kicked at the man's shins.

His hand reached for his sword. Atarah tightened her grip around his neck and screamed, "Go! Run! Find Imma!"

She was none too confident Havah, the little warrior, would obey. But she must have heard something in Atarah's tone or seen it in her face—or perhaps the enormity of the situation overwhelmed her courage. She took off at a run, shouting over her shoulder. "I will get help!"

As if there was any help for them now but from the Lord. These were Syrians attacking them, they must be. They were the only raiders plaguing Israel just now—but she had not thought they would reach them all the way here in Ramah. Along the borders, yes, of course. But they were not in Jezreel or Megiddo or Mount Tabor. They were in the heart of the land, mere miles from Jerusalem. If this army had come all this way, they must be a large force. Well trained.

A school of men and boys more skilled in prayer than war would never stand a chance against them, unless the Lord fought for them.

But the Lord *could* fight for them. Perhaps He *would*. Her eyes caught one of the many frantic movements going on around her, and she recognized it with a sudden gush of faith. Gehazi. Her father's oldest friend was rushing between the buildings, which meant that Elisha was here, or nearby. And if the prophet was here, that meant hope. "Gehazi! Help!" He could call down power from on high, surely. He was the prophet's aide, closer to him than anyone.

He must not have heard her over the clamor. Though he glanced her way, he could not have seen her. Had he seen her, heard her, he would not have run the opposite direction. He would have helped.

Something slashed her arm, a thousand bees stinging. Though she told herself to hang on despite it, her arms disobeyed. They loosened a bit, just enough for the man to suck in a mighty breath. The next thing she knew, she was flying through the air again, cartwheeling, the ground slapping her back and kicking the air from her lungs. Her vision blurred around the edges, spots of light dancing before her eyes.

And heat. Heat seared her, scorched her, crackled in her ears. The man had tossed her terrifyingly near to the burning building.

Though it was not half as terrifying as the look on his face as he stalked toward her, a short sword gripped in his hand, tinged red.

She tried to move, to roll, to leap to her feet, but her body refused to obey her. Her lungs could not inflate, gasp as she might for air.

He was going to kill her. She saw it in the blaze of hatred in his eyes, this man she had never seen until he tried to steal away her sister. He would plunge that sword into her chest and kill her here and now.

Would it hurt? Would she reclaim enough breath to cry out, or would she go silently into the bosom of Abraham? Did Yahweh's angels, the host of heavenly warriors, sing? Would she be permitted to greet her Lord with her voice?

"Atarah!"

The voice pounded through the haze of her mind in the same moment that her eyes registered movement. Someone leaped between her and the advancing Syrian, a long, smooth stick in his hands—a garden tool, nothing more—held up like a weapon or a shield.

Tavi. He must have gotten the boys to safety with Imma and heard Havah shout that she needed help. He crouched now in the stance the boys always took up when they were sparring, ready for an attack.

But it was no wooden sword in the soldier's hands.

Atarah, finally able to pull air back into her chest, rolled onto her stomach. She had to get up. To help Tavi. To check on her family. To do *something* other than lie here like a victim. She braced her hands against the earth, but then there was a crash. A *whoosh* of hot air. Crushing pain in her ankle.

She let out a yell without thinking, following it with a prayer that it would not distract Tavi. A glance his way told her the Syrian had reached him and that Tavi was parrying the blows of his sword with that garden tool. It could not withstand the attack long, surely.

*Yahweh Nissi, God my banner, protect him, please!*

Her ankle throbbed with pain, stealing her attention. The roof of the burning building had collapsed, pulling part of the structure down with it. A beam had fallen, tumbled through the doorway, and now pinned her to the spot.

It was not ablaze, at least. Yet. If she could only escape the weight...

A cry from Tavi. She looked his way again, afraid to breathe. But he had not been run through, simply knocked to the ground. And the raider's gaze had reset on *her.*

The reason was no doubt linked to the red welts on his face. Had she done that? She had no recollection of scratching him, but she must have. When he was tossing her, perhaps.

"No!" She lifted a hand, as if that would provide her any protection. "Please!"

"Ram! Stop!" The new voice worked the miracle of stopping the raider's advance. Ram? Was that his name? The voice spoke in a dialect that sounded at once foreign to her ears, and yet she managed to untangle it. The owner of the voice strode through the smoke, a sword in his hands and authority about his shoulders as surely as his cloak.

The first Syrian lowered his sword, but the gleam in his eyes did not abate. "General?"

*General?* The man in charge of this raid, then. He came directly to Atarah, peering down at her from what seemed a very great height. Or perhaps it was just because she was pinned to the ground. "You, girl." He spoke slowly, as if aware that it took her a moment to process the odd inflections of his words. "You were the one singing?"

Her brows knit. He had heard her? Of course he had heard her. They must have been in position outside the walls the whole time she sang. But why would he care? "Yes."

Something odd flitted through his eyes. Something that, had she seen it in her father's eyes, or Tavi's or Imma's or Elisha's or Gehazi's, she would have labeled *peace*. But that could not be so, certainly not here and now, with the school in ruins around her, their bountiful crop parading away on the backs of quick-footed Syrians even now.

He nodded and, with what looked like minimal effort, levered the now-smoldering beam off her ankle. "I thought so. You will come with me."

She jerked her leg free and leaped to her feet. In her mind's eye, she saw herself running away, helping Tavi to his feet again on her way by. Both of them darting to freedom.

Her ankle buckled the moment she put weight on it, and she would have fallen directly back to the ground had the general not grasped her arm. "Easy, little one. You will hurt yourself more."

As if he cared—as if physical pain could possibly compare to the terror his words had struck in her heart. "No. No, I will not. I will not go anywhere!" She pulled against his arm, struggled, flailed, shouted.

Tavi had regained his feet and was charging toward them, his face a mask of desperation. "No! Atarah!"

He stumbled and fell forward, the furious-faced Ram but a step behind, clearly the reason for Tavi's stumble. He raised his sword again.

"No." The general held up a hand, that strange, calm gaze on Tavi now. "Do not kill him, Ram. Take him too. That one has the soul of a warrior."

"That is why he should be killed, General."

Atarah froze. Ram held the tip of his sword to Tavi's back. She would do nothing to convince him to plunge it in, to convince the general to agree with him.

The general shook his head. "I said you will not. These two—they will be my prizes. Sami! Miran!"

Two more soldiers had appeared through the smoke billowing over the compound, snapping to attention at their general's call. He motioned to Atarah and then to Tavi. "Bind these two and take them to the caravan. And be gentle with the girl. She is injured. She will require a mount."

*Gentle?* He bade his men be *gentle* with her, when they had just set her home on fire, stolen the fruit of their labors, and were now stealing her away from her family? Well, if they obeyed, then she would take advantage of it. She would fight, she would lunge away. She would...what? What could she do while Ram still held his blade to Tavi? Any sudden move on her part, and she had the dread certainty that he would seize the excuse to kill her friend. He could simply claim that he reacted before he could think.

No. She would not endanger Tavi's life, not after he had risked his for her.

He was rising slowly, no doubt keenly aware of the tip of the sword. He held his hands out from his sides. His gaze moved over her, paused on the throbbing ankle, and then settled on the man holding her captive. "May I stay with her, General?"

The general looked amused. "Of course. As long as you both behave yourselves."

Tavi's arms were tugged down by one of the newcomers, a length of rope soon appearing to bind his hands behind his back. The other soldier moved behind her and soon wrestled her arms in compliance as well.

"Gently. I have plans for this one."

Her stomach was a stone, heavy and hard and gagging. She had no idea what plans he might have—but she knew they would be horrifying. Whimpering, she sought Tavi's eyes again. They could lunge, make a move in unison....

He gave a small shake of his head, those serious, water-blue eyes bidding her stay calm.

He was right, of course. They would be killed if they tried anything now. They would have to go quietly. And then sneak away under cover of darkness.

But escape they must. Because there was no way she meant to go to Syria as this man's slave and wait to see what *plans* he had for her.

# CHAPTER THREE

Dusk had fallen over the land, and miles had fallen away underfoot. Atarah wanted to moan with pain—from her ankle, from sore arms bound to the saddle, from sitting in said saddle all day without reprieve. But she would not give utterance to a single complaint. Not when Tavi had trudged the entire distance on foot beside her, his arms also bound to her saddle. Not when a veritable sea of Syrians surrounded them, looking at them as though they were just two more heads of cattle or sheep.

Not when she must prove to them all that the people of Israel deserved respect.

Despair, though, nipped at her heels as the sea of horses, carts, and soldiers finally ground to a halt. How far had they come? Farther than she had ever gone before. How would they find their way home again? She had tried to note landmarks, but this was far different from an afternoon's walk through the olive grove.

Tavi stepped closer to the horse she had been riding—a huge, snorting monster that she had expected to buck her off at any moment. She had never even been so near a horse. And then to ride one for hours on end? It had taken half the day for the terror to ease up even a bit. Horses were for battle or for kings. Not for injured songbirds. She would have done better with a donkey or an ox. Or even a wooly sheep.

Tavi exhibited no nerves, though. He even ran his bound hands down the horse's shoulder.

"Tavi." She had so much to say to him that she had not dared give voice to as they trudged northward. Questions to ask. Forgiveness to beg. Plans to forge. He looked up at her. "What will we do?" She kept her voice so low a whisper that he might not have even heard her over the bustle of a hundred men making camp.

His hands clasped her uninjured foot. A connection that, under different circumstances, would have been amusing. Or odd. Now, it sent a trickle of comfort into her heart. "Whatever Yahweh Shammah asks of us."

Yahweh Shammah—*the Lord Is There.* Even here, in the midst of a Syrian camp. He was here, He saw them. She knew it was true.

But what of His prophets? Were they alive, back at the school in Ramah? Or had the soldiers murdered them all? Her parents? Her siblings? Gehazi and the prophet? Why had He not warned them, given one of His servants a vision? Why had such destruction struck them? Struck *her?*

The glowering Syrian who had held the reins to her horse all day appeared behind Tavi. "General Naaman wishes to see you both."

It was the first she had heard the name of the general. She stored it in her mind and made no argument when the man untied their ropes from the saddle and pulled her from the horse. With a bit of luck, she would never have to come near such a creature again.

Her knees buckled when her feet hit the ground, her legs too weak to hold her—and her ankle screaming at the weight she tried to put on it. Tavi must have anticipated her weakness though, because his arm had come up under hers to catch her, steady her.

She sent him a strained smile in thanks.

"Hurry." The soldier tugged on the ropes he held, which nearly sent her sprawling.

Tavi gripped her rope in his bound hands. "She is injured—she cannot walk unaided. May I help her? If you would permit me to put my arms around her, or carry her..."

She frowned, more at his tone than his suggestion. He spoke with humble respect. Not groveling, not begging, but deference filling his words. The exact way he always spoke to her father. To the other teachers at the school.

How could he possibly bring himself to offer the same to this Syrian soldier? When these people—or their comrades, at any rate—had killed his parents? Destroyed his home? Taken everything of worth before and now had struck again?

It was effective though. The soldier hesitated only a moment before nodding. "Carry her, it will be quicker. The general wants to speak with you before his meal, and it will be ready soon."

And would the general be feasting on *their* harvest? Their livestock? Atarah gritted her teeth together while Tavi scooped her into the circle of his arms and lifted her. It must be awkward for him, unable as he was to move his wrists apart, but his face betrayed no unease. She slid her own arm-circle over his head to add some extra stability.

"I am sorry, Tavi," she whispered as they began moving.

His eyes sought hers. "For what?"

"Everything." Her throat was so tight, as if she had been singing for hours—but it was the fight against tears that strained her, not the echo of melodies. "If you had not come to my rescue, you would have gotten to safety. And you must be exhausted, but still you must carry me."

Had anyone ever had a truer friend?

His eyes softened, though his lips made no effort to turn up. She could hardly blame him now. "Do not apologize for that. I did it—*do* it—willingly."

"But..." She squeezed her eyes shut, the images from that morning bombarding her mind again. "My family. Do you know if they were safe?"

His breath whispered out. "I had just delivered the boys to your mother when Havah came up screaming that someone had you. I did not pause to see if they made it to the cellar in safety."

Because he had come to help her. But at least she knew the rest of the children were together, with Imma. She had to believe they had escaped. She had to.

At the very least, she could verify that they were not here in this swarm of raiders. Over the course of the day she had cataloged every Hebrew she could find with her gaze, and though there were other captives in the group, she recognized none from the school. There was a lad from Ramah she had seen before, and a woman of middling years whom she vaguely recalled seeing at a festival. But the rest must have come from other villages throughout Israel, collected before the raid on the school.

Perhaps it had been the last raid, for they were heading north now without question. Back toward Syria.

How many of her people had they killed though? How much of their provisions had they stolen?

They drew near to a large tent at the head of the group. Its flap was up, but the soldier leading them halted Tavi with a raised hand and stepped into, but not through, the opening. "General Naaman—here they are, my lord."

"Excellent. Bring them in."

Tavi must have sensed that she would not want to face their captor in such a weak position. He lowered her carefully back to her feet, merely offering his arm to lean on as they stepped slowly into the lamp-lit interior.

She frowned at the inside of the tent before she could think to stop herself. It must have been put up quickly, but even so it was extravagant. The walls were rich, thick cloth woven with a colorful design. Rugs had been laid out on the ground and a table set up, overflowing with scrolls. Cushions in red and yellow shouted that this was a man of wealth, enough of it that he apparently did not mind bringing some with him while he waged war.

He looked up from the scroll in his hands and smiled at them—no, *beamed*. As if he was pleased to see them and expected the same pleasure in return.

Atarah lifted her chin.

Tavi dipped his. "My lord. You asked to see us?"

"I did. Sit, please, before the maiden collapses." He motioned to the nearest cushions, and Tavi helped her over to them. She would have preferred to stand, out of defiance if nothing else, but she would not fight Tavi, and he was easing her down into the pillows' soft embrace and then sitting beside her.

Naaman took a seat too, across from them. His gaze arrowed into Atarah. "Please, do not be frightened. I mean you no harm. How is your foot?"

She pressed her lips together.

Tavi cleared his throat. "Her ankle is swollen badly, my lord. I saw several lacerations, as well as bruising and swelling."

The general frowned. "I will have salve and wrappings brought to you, so you can bind it for her. Your names?"

"Tavi, son of Elah. And she is Atarah, daughter of Johash."

Had she not been so far in Tavi's debt, she would have jabbed an elbow into his side in objection.

"Tavi and Atarah." Naaman nodded. "You will both join my household, and you will find other Hebrews there to welcome you."

Previously stolen away, he meant. She folded her arms over her chest. They would escape long before they left Israelite territory.

"It is a good house—you will be well cared for." He smiled, as if he were showering blessings down upon them instead of curses. "I can promise that you will never want, never go hungry again."

Again? What did he think, that they were all starving in Israel? Preposterous—though if ever they *did* go hungry, it was likely because men like him had stolen their grain.

His gaze settled on her again. It was a heavy thing but not unkind. Which only made her angrier. How could this man look at her in the same way her father did, when he was a killer, not a prophet? A Syrian? "Your voice...I knew the moment I heard you sing this morning that I must find you."

She stiffened, her throat going tight again. "I beg your pardon?"

"My son." He closed his eyes briefly. "He is often troubled in spirit, the poor little thing. A lullaby soothes him as nothing else, but my wife..." He shook his head. "She can barely speak above a whisper, much less sing. An old injury. But you, Atarah— you can be her voice. She will welcome you as her maidservant with all joy."

Her nostrils flared. He had been looking for her in particular? He had...had targeted her because of her voice? Her singing?

*Why, Yahweh? The very thing I use to praise You! Why would You allow that to be my undoing?* Had she taken too much pride in her singing? She had always tried to guard against it, to remember always that her voice, if pleasant, was so only because God had given it to her. Only because she was meant to use it for His glory.

But she must have failed. She must have done something wrong.

One thing she knew though—she would never sing for this man or his family. Never.

"And you, Tavi." Naaman turned his gaze on him with an easy smile. "I admire the courage you demonstrated today when Atarah was in danger. I believe in rewarding such courage. How would you like to be trained as a bodyguard for my wife and children? And hence for your friend, of course. And I would educate you as well, if you wish it."

Tavi dipped his head. "I would be honored, my lord."

Had he gone mad? Atarah blinked at him. No—no, not Tavi. He was playing a part. That must be it. A show of deference, of humility. It would gain trust. Perhaps they would not be guarded so strictly. Then they could make their escape.

A wiser plan than her own stubborn silence, in all likelihood.

"Good." But Naaman sounded troubled. Perhaps he had seen through the ruse. Certainly Tavi must have thought so, because he looked up again, met the general's eyes. Naaman shook his head. "You have the most remarkable eyes. I cannot help but think...but you are from Ramah."

Something cold and hard settled in her chest.

Tavi sucked in a long breath. "Not originally. My family was from Jezreel."

"Jezreel." The Syrian's eyes narrowed. "I led a raid on Jezreel some years ago. Two? No, three. It was just before I met Ramina. I saw a boy there with your eyes."

Tavi's fingers curled into his palms. "You must have seen me, my lord."

"No." Atarah did not mean to let the horror seep out in that word, but it was too great to be restrained. Too unfair. Too cruel.

The very ones—the very man who had led *that* raid, leading this one too? The one responsible for the deaths of Tavi's parents, now responsible for him being taken captive? How could Tavi even keep his limbs calm, his chin level? How could he keep from screaming, lashing out, flying at this man? The very general who had killed his parents, leading him away captive! Daring to speak of blessing and liking and impressions?

But Tavi merely drew in a long, long breath through his nostrils.

Naaman let out a mirroring one. "I am sorry. I can imagine the tragedy that led you so far from your home, then. These raids...they are the command of my king. But I always instruct my men to spare life whenever possible."

Atarah snorted. From what she knew of the Syrians, that was the opposite of their usual ways. They were ruthless, the lot of them. They always hovered over the borderlands, striking terror into the hearts of any who lived under their shadow.

There was no possible way this man had risen to the rank of general by his age—he could not be more than forty, if that—by being *kind*. No—he would have risen by being the *most* ruthless. Which meant this was only a clever ploy. A deception to try to win their trust and get them to go along passively, easily.

Tavi nodded, his larynx bobbing with a hard swallow—the only indication that he felt more than he showed. "And we thank you for sparing us today, my lord. When your man wanted to kill us both."

A shudder coursed up Atarah's spine. That much was true. The one called Ram would have killed them both had Naaman not stepped in.

"Ram." The curve of Naaman's lips could hardly be called a smile. "You will want to be watchful any time he is near. He is my wife's cousin, and he is often assigned to my service, but he is most assuredly *not* 'my man.' He will not forget that I robbed him of the pleasure of your blood."

Another shudder. Ram, at least, fit her idea of these heartless raiders. Which gave her no comfort whatsoever. Not only were they captives, slaves, but they already had an enemy who would happily kill them still. That was what this man was saying.

"Sami." Though his voice had been only half a measure louder than before, a soldier appeared in the open flap, clearly having been waiting for the summons. Naaman motioned to them. "Take Tavi and Atarah to the other captives and see they are well fed. And bring salve and wrappings for the young woman's injuries, then loose Tavi's bonds so he can tend her. I will not have my wife's new handmaiden losing a foot or dying of infection before we reach Damascus."

"Yes, General."

Atarah made no complaint as Tavi helped her back to her feet and then picked her up again the moment they were back outside. Her mind whirled. There was too much to process, too much to plan. But if they were going to unbind Tavi's hands... they would no doubt keep a close watch on them while he was free, yes. But he could perhaps loosen hers, enough that she could then free them both once night fell fully. They could make their escape—now, before they were led any farther from home.

"Still those thoughts, my friend," he murmured as they approached the place where the other Hebrew captives had settled onto the hard ground and were devouring what looked like a paltry ration of food, barely enough to keep them alive another day. "I know what you are thinking—but it is too dangerous."

She huffed out a breath as he lowered her to the ground in the place Sami indicated. While the guard vanished, presumably in search of medical supplies, she whispered back, "It is our best chance. Before we get any farther away."

"You think they do not know this? That guards will not be extra vigilant?"

Of course they would. And if they were caught trying to escape, she had a feeling Naaman's desire to put her in a cage, a songbird for his wife and son, would matter little. They would be killed. Or worse. "We must try."

"We must *not*."

"Tavi—"

"Atarah, *please.*" He reached his bound hands for hers and leaned close. His eyes, the color of water, sparked with flame. "Trust me. Trust me to protect you."

She did—of *course* she did. How could she not, when he had sacrificed his own freedom for her? But... "I do not want to be a slave. I do not want *you* to be a prisoner to the very man responsible for your parents' deaths. How can you bear it? Even another minute?"

Sami strode their way again, effectively silencing them. He did not linger long at their side, though. After depositing bandages, salve, and food, he simply released Tavi's hands, grunted something about the guard a few feet away being the best archer among them, and vanished again.

Tavi sat at her feet then lifted her injured one carefully into his lap and removed her sandal. Though as gentle as possible, each touch sent new pain shooting up her leg.

There was no way she would be able to run out of this camp or walk home. Logically, she knew that. But Yahweh Rapha was the God who healed. He could make her well. He could deliver them. He *could*, if only He chose to.

Tavi poured something over the cuts and scrapes that made them burn like a wildfire. She bit down hard to keep from screaming.

He glanced up at her. "God is our refuge. A very present help in danger. Do you believe this, Atarah?"

Tears had gathered unbidden in her eyes in the wake of the pain. Still, she nodded. She had sung those words just yesterday—before she knew how near the danger was.

"He is the Lord of the angel armies. The God who sees. The Lord our Banner. The Almighty and the Creator, the Lord who provides and is there. *Here.* He is our Shepherd."

All the names for their Lord that she had learned at Abba's knees, in Imma's arms. Not daring to open her mouth lest her pain come pouring out, she nodded.

He dabbed soothing, sticky honey onto her wounds. But his eyes were not focused on her damaged ankle. They were focused on hers. And they were alight with the flame she had seen before, in other eyes.

In Abba's. In Elisha's. In Gehazi's. The Light of God, of His Spirit.

She shuddered again but not with horror. Not this time.

Tavi's hands stilled. "He is also Yahweh Shalom—our peace. And He is here, in this situation. His hand is on us. Do you believe this?"

Did she? She should. But how could she, now? The Lord had warned His people that their disobedience would lead them to be taken captive—so did that mean she had disobeyed? That she misunderstood Him? What if all she thought she knew, that she believed, was a mistake?

The only words she could whisper were, "I *want* to believe it."

"Then do. Cling to His promises and be who He created you to be. Trust that this, even this, is part of His purpose."

Who He created her to be...but how? How could she sing His praises in a pagan, foreign land?

Tavi wrapped her ankle, tightly enough to support but careful not to cut off the flow of blood.

She did not deserve such tender care. "Tavi..." She waited for him to look at her again. The Light had dimmed in his gaze, but it was still warm from it. Familiar. The only rock she had right now. "I am sorry. Sorry you are here because of me."

The corners of his lips pulled up in one of his rare, priceless smiles. He handed her a hunk of bread. "I am not."

"But you must be. These are the people who killed your parents."

He offered her a date and then took one for himself and a little bread. He scooted up to her side and gazed out over the company now. "They did. And it has taken me three years to learn how to forgive them. But God has worked that miracle in me—because when I looked at the general...I did not see the man who led the raid that killed my parents, Atarah. I saw the man who spared my life then. And who spared it again today." He turned, met her eye. "Twice the Lord has put me in his path. I do not know why. But I will serve him with loyalty."

He was a better person, a more devoted follower of the Most High than she could ever hope to be. Or a raving lunatic. She looked down at the bread clasped in her bound hands. "I just want to go home."

"You will. Eventually. I will return you to our people, my friend. I give you my word."

She sneaked a glance at him, searching for that Light of prophecy again, but he kept his gaze focused on his dinner. She could not tell if it was truth or merely hope that he spoke. With a sigh, she raised the date to her lips and tore off a bite of its sweet flesh.

The last glow of the sun faded into the horizon, night's dark blanket settling over them. She tilted her head back, searching for the first star, a point of light to pierce the darkness. But if it was there, she could not see it through the sheen of tears clouding her eyes again.

"Is it too much to ask of you to sing for me?" His words came quietly now, hesitantly.

A sob caught in her throat. She wanted to give him that—to give him the hope he had tried to give her. To remind him of the faithfulness of God he had never for a moment forgotten. But she could think of no melodies. No tunes. No notes. She could call to mind no words of Him, either of sorrow or desperation or rage or praise.

A torch was coming their way, illuminating the face of Sami. No doubt set on retying Tavi's hands.

He sighed and positioned them on his raised knees in offering. "No matter. You will sing again, when the Lord gives you a new song."

Would she? Just now she could not imagine such a thing. Music had always been water to her, refreshment, life. But her soul was a parched and barren land tonight. And she was no prophet. She could not imagine a day when it would be any different.

# CHAPTER FOUR

They had been in the territory of Aram-Damascus for days already. Atarah had given up counting. One trudged into the next, marked by the scorching late-summer sun during the day and the cool winds promising winter at night. Her foot had healed. Her heart had not. If anything, it had solidified. Turned to rock with hardness rivaling that of the stones making up the wall now before them. *Damascus.* Her prison.

She eased a little closer to Tavi's side as the city loomed ever nearer. It was far larger than Ramah, its walls menacing. The roads leading to its gates were all bustling with people and animals and carts.

Their own procession was halted outside the city, clear of said roads and gates. No explanation was offered to the captives, but it required no great mental acuity to understand that the general would be reporting to the king. This great sea of prizes—her people, their produce, their animals—would be divvied up. Sold. Dispersed.

Her hands gripped the rope by which she was tied to Tavi on one side, the lad from Ramah on the other. Her wrists had gone raw in the first few days, then healed, scarred, and calloused.

She and Tavi had been treated better than most of the captives though, so she had no room to complain. They had been given salve for their injuries, plus better food than the others, and more of it. And once they were far enough from home that neither of them could possibly get back, they even enjoyed occasional moments free of the ropes altogether.

Naaman had been keeping his promise that they would be cared for. But he was still their new master. They were still his slaves. If he expected gratitude, he would have better luck getting it from the stones than from her.

She missed her parents. Her siblings. Her friends. Missed them with an ache so deep it felt sometimes as though it would split her in two. If not for Tavi by her side, she surely would have cracked to pieces.

Worse though was the silence in her soul. Day after endless, footsore day, the silence had only deepened. If there was any music left in the world, she could not find it.

No...she could not even try to look for it. Her ears had been stopped up by the constant clopping of hooves and marching feet. But it was more than that. More than her ears. The problem was with her heart. That was where the melodies and harmonies had always come from. And that was the part of her being most damaged by the endless journey away from home.

"It will not be so bad." Tavi spoke the words for her alone, softly. His gaze wandered over every inch they could see of Damascus. "The Lord will watch over us."

His unflagging optimism alternately comforted and chafed. Today, it was as abrasive as the ropes. She made no reply.

After two hours of standing still outside the gates, movement seized the camp again. People came from the city and began breaking bits of their caravan off. Officials, probably. Perhaps traders. At first she simply watched as sheep and cattle were led away, as carts of provisions were steered toward the gates. But then strange men approached the group of captives, and her back went stiff. Something about the way their gazes shifted over them, measuring and gauging, made her certain they were slave traders.

And each set of their eyes rested time and again on her and Tavi.

She shrank into his side, suddenly not so glad that they had been well fed. They had tried, at first, to share their portions with the others, but the guards had not allowed it. They could sneak bits here and there but not enough to really make a difference. Not enough to keep themselves from standing out now.

Panic sank its fangs into her. Many times over their march they had been called into Naaman's tent. He told them about his family, even taught them a bit of the history of his people. She had stubbornly refused to like him—but she would take his kind eyes over these shadowed ones any day. Where was he though? What was to stop these men from taking them, selling them, separating them?

"Tavi." She reached for his hands.

Their fingers tangled together. "It is all right. The general was too determined to find you for his wife to let you be taken away now."

But the general answered to the king. And what if Ben-Hadad had forbidden him from keeping any of the captives for himself? Did such a thing ever happen? She had no idea. But those dreadful men were coming closer. Closer still.

One reached out and grasped her chin. "Pretty enough," he said in that dialect that had become all too familiar during the journey. "How old are you, girl?"

She would have preferred spitting in his face to answering him, but she lacked the courage. "Fifteen." Where was Naaman?

The trader sneered, eyes glinting with dark light. "She will fetch a high price. Do you not agree, Mardeen?"

Another trader laughed. "Indeed. I know a priest who would—"

"Not those two." Another man elbowed his way forward. Atarah did not recognize him, but in that moment she could have embraced him. "General Naaman has claimed them already. Untie them—the girl and this young man here."

A guard stepped forward to obey.

Minutes later, the stranger was leading her and Tavi away from the others. While still around the crowds, he said nothing. But once they had stepped clear of the masses, he pointed to a house situated against the eastern wall, so grand she wondered if it was the palace of the king.

"That is Naaman's home, where you will both serve." He offered them a smile. "I am Seena—the head of the general's guard. I will be training you, Tavi."

Tavi nodded. Atarah was too busy studying the house—and particularly the figures she could just make out on the rooftop moving about in what looked to be a game. For the first time, she paused to wonder what this new mistress—this Ramina—was actually like. The general described her as sweet and loving, but those were the words of a clearly doting husband. Women were all too often different when out of their husbands' company.

"My impressions of the general," Tavi said, "is that he is a fair master. We are blessed and grateful to serve in his house."

Seena chuckled, and it sounded like any free man's chuckle. Unhindered by the invisible shackles he wore as a slave as surely as they did. "You will swiftly see that our father is better than fair, my young friend. He is merciful and gracious. He treats even the lowliest maid as if she is a member of his family. There is truly no better house in all of Aram to be a part of."

In all of Aram, perhaps. But her own abba's house, where she *was* a member of a family, was by nature preferable.

As they walked, the figures on the roof became more clearly people—a woman with long hair that swung around her as she darted this way and that, in chase of a little boy who toddled about with waving arms. The walls were high enough that she could see only the top of the little one's head and those excited hands, until the mother scooped him and held him high before putting him down for the next round of the game.

Baby laughter drifted to her ears on the breeze, and then they were too close to see them anymore. Soon they were *there*, being led through a door and along a corridor, then back outside to a courtyard and its kitchen.

"Dafna! I have brought you two new chicks for your flock."
Seena shouted the greeting with a smile in his voice before
Atarah had even stepped into the kitchen.

She had to look around only for a moment before she spotted the woman who must be Dafna. She was about the age of
Atarah's grandmother, with wrinkles around her eyes that
attested to many smiles just like the one she wore now. Given
her name and features, she was likely a Hebrew too. Naaman
had said he owned others, so that was no surprise.

The woman surged forward, arms extended like the toddler's on the roof had been. "Oh, you poor darlings! What a
journey you would have had—but I trust our father saw that
you were well cared for during it."

Dafna's arms closed around Atarah. She smelled of bread
and honey and yogurt and fruit—she smelled of Imma. She
smelled of *home.* It made tears sting Atarah's eyes and her arms
squeeze the woman back before she could remind herself that
this was not where she wanted to be, this woman not the one
she wanted embracing her.

"There now," she whispered into Atarah's ear. "I know. I
remember. But the Most High sees us here as He does in Israel,
my precious girl. Your life is no less in His palm."

Could she read hearts and minds? Atarah sniffled and
then stepped back. She dug up a smile. "Thank you."

Dafna's warm hand settled on her cheek. "What is your
name, child?"

"Atarah."

"*Crown.*" Dafna gave a decisive nod. "It suits you. A beautiful name for a beautiful young woman. And who is this strapping young man with you?" She turned to face Tavi, drawing him into her home-scented hug even as he answered her.

Atarah's heart stuttered. How was it possible that she had spent the entire journey here hardening her heart, determined to hate everything about this place...yet within a few minutes, she had gone from resentful to—to—whatever this feeling was? Not exactly accepting but grateful that it was Naaman and not those slave traders who had claimed her. Softened by the laughter of a mother and child on the roof. Comforted by the welcome of one of her own.

After Dafna had released Tavi, Seema clapped a hand to his shoulder. "I will show you to the barracks where all the unmarried menservants live and where we will train. Dafna will do the same for Atarah. You will see each other at every meal, and often enough otherwise, especially once you have completed a bit of training. The general said he means to assign you to protect the mistress and the children."

Another of Tavi's solemn nods. "I will be glad to do so."

She wanted to grab his arm, beg him not to leave her side—he never had, not once during the weeks of their journey. Instead she tucked her hands behind her back and offered him what she hoped was a brave smile. Never in a lifetime could she adequately thank him for being such a friend to her. But she would be grateful that they were still together and that she could try.

"Come, my dear one." Dafna motioned toward another woman in the corner whom Atarah had failed to notice, waving her toward the cook fire. "Panna will tend things here while I show you around. You will be serving our lady, Seena said?"

Atarah found her head bobbing. "That is what the general tells me."

"Then you will have no need to know many of the inner workings of the kitchen. Though in her current condition," she said with a chuckle, "the mistress *does* frequently require unscheduled snacks. So I will show you where we keep the food itself."

"She is with child?" Atarah had lived through enough pregnancies of Imma's to know what to expect.

"Praise Yahweh, yes." Dafna indicated bowls of fruit, bars made of pressed grains and dates and spices, bread—Ramina's favorites, apparently. "The master's first wife was a lovely woman—we all adored her—but in ten years of marriage, she never carried a child to term. We mourned terribly with him when the last loss took her with it." Indeed, grief saturated her tone. "But that was five years ago. We were all thrilled when he brought our sweet new mistress home and beyond thrilled when little Malak was born, healthy and vibrant. Our lord has proven himself as doting a father as we all knew he would be, and he will be ecstatic when he learns another little one will join the family."

Dafna led her into another corridor, pointing out the rooms where the master and mistress entertained, where they ate, where each of them liked to spend certain hours. "The maids' rooms are through here. Small, of course, but our father is generous with his allowances—you will have a cot of your own, new clothing. You will share the space with Panna, and I know you will get along well."

Atarah peeked into the room she indicated—it was no smaller than the one she shared with the twins at home.

"Now"—Dafna wove their arms together and led her onward, toward the stairs—"if you are anything like me when I first arrived in this land, you will not like what you will see next. My family was always faithful to Yahweh. No idols were ever permitted in our home."

Idols? Of course there would be idols—even in Israel, as Dafna hinted, there were plenty who kept them. But she shuddered a bit at the very thought. "My father is one of the prophets at the School of the Sons of the Prophets in Ramah." She clung to that *is*—he had to be alive, she would not let herself believe otherwise. "Such abominations certainly never crossed our threshold either."

"Good. But of course, things are different here. They call their god Rimmon, but it is just another name for Ba'al." Dafna led her to a little nook set into the wall at the bottom of the stairs. A recessed ledge, with a silver figure upon it. "What do you see?"

She had been planning on averting her eyes, rushing past. At Dafna's question, she started. But then she looked more closely.

The little statue was the only thing there. No offerings molded and fermented, no incense left ash around it, as she had heard was common. A layer of dust even covered the silver statue. She frowned. "It is in disuse."

Dafna nodded. "We clean it when the king is coming—but only then. Our master is the favorite of the king and goes with him regularly to the temple of Rimmon. The king even leans upon him for support! But he has never been an ardent follower. His first wife was, which is why the idol is silver, well crafted. But Ramina..." Dafna shook her head. "She refuses to give even lip-service to Rimmon. Not after what happened to her in his name."

For the second time, curiosity pricked her about this woman who would be her mistress. What had happened? She nearly asked. Probably would have, had quick footsteps not drawn her attention to the stairs.

The young woman who appeared must have been Ramina— her clothes were too fine to belong to a maid, not to mention the gold and jewels she wore. But that was where Atarah's expectations failed to meet reality. The woman's eyes were not haughty—they were simply delighted. Her face was not set in a scowl but in a grin. The toddler on her hip did not fuss and whine at the moment but still giggled with that baby chortle that tugged matching smiles to other lips by sheer magnetism. The lady could not be more than a few years older than Atarah. And she looked upon her as though she were a long-lost friend instead of a captive slave.

"Atarah?" Ramina rushed forward, a hand extended. Her voice was little more than a throaty whisper. "My husband said that is your name. How beautiful!"

In the next moment, Atarah's fingers were clasped by Ramina's, and the little one was clapping pudgy hands and trying to say her name too.

One of the stones she had so carefully erected around her heart cracked and crumbled. She should probably dip her knees in a show of respect, or at least bow her head. But instead she smiled at the little one. "Thank you. And what is this little fellow's name?"

"Malak." Ramina kissed the top of his head. "And I am Ramina. Come." She extended her free hand, still grinning. "Let me show you where we spend most of our time."

Atarah held up her own hand and let Ramina clasp it. Her head swam for a single moment, frozen in time. Her friends in Ramah had acted this very way. Smiling, giggling, holding hands and tugging each other this way and that. But Ramina was not her friend. Ramina *owned* her—or her husband did. It was different.

It *had* to be different. So why did it feel so strangely similar?

Ramina led her up the stairs with Dafna following. A minute later the lady led them into a large room, sunlight spilling in and painting everything in bright tones. The chamber was as large as Atarah's entire house in Ramah—as big as the sanctuary the students all met in at the school when the weather was ill-suited for gathering in the courtyard.

"This is where I spend most of my day. Here or up on the roof," Ramina whispered. Malak lunged for the floor, and she put him on his feet, smiling as he toddled off toward a basket of wooden blocks. "I am so grateful to have a companion to share the hours with me again." She met Atarah's gaze, her own bright and joyful. "My previous maid married and joined her husband's household. I asked Naaman to let her, but I did not realize how much I would miss her!"

For lack of a better response, Atarah nodded. And nearly frowned when she caught sight of an ugly scar on Ramina's neck. She had not noticed it before, given Malak's presence on his mother's torso, but now it glared at her. Did it have something to do with her lack of voice? An injury?

Ramina settled to a seat on a wide cushion and motioned for Atarah and Dafna to do the same. "Please. Have some refreshment." She nodded toward a tall pitcher and a few metal cups.

Atarah would have just stared at it, perhaps sniffed, but Dafna had no such hesitation. She poured three cups and handed one to each of them.

Fruit juice, Atarah realized with the first sip. Unfermented. Probably freshly squeezed by Dafna's own hand, so of course she had known exactly what it was.

Atarah savored her first mouthful. After a long journey with only water and rations, this tasted like something straight from Eden.

"Mistress, you must be so relieved that the master has returned safely." Dafna sat down as well, defying yet another of Atarah's preconceptions. What sort of mistress invited her maid and her cook to relax with her?

Ramina's expression spoke far more loudly than her voice. She pressed a hand to her chest. "Even when the army was spotted, I could not quite erase my fears. I hate knowing Ram is there with him."

Atarah nearly choked on her next sip of juice. Ramina distrusted Ram too?

The lady did not miss her splutter. "I see you have had some interaction with my cousin, to react so."

Her nostrils flared. "He tried to kill me."

Ramina touched a hand to the scar on her throat. "Then we have much in common. Had Naaman not come to my rescue, I have no doubt Ram would have done more than damage my throat as he cried out to Rimmon in a drunken rage." A violent shudder shook her, made her wince.

Atarah very nearly put the cup down and went to comfort her. She would have, had it been a friend or sister or Imma. "Why would he do such a thing to you?"

"I told him he had imbibed enough and tried to deny him another cup of wine." Though she shrugged, her eyes belied the casualness of the gesture. But they brightened when a smile crept over her lips. "Though it was this that introduced me to Naaman. So I cannot regret it."

A great clatter came from the basket of blocks, followed by a tired-sounding toddler scream.

"Malak!" The whisper held a rebuke, but it was too quiet to penetrate through the scream. Ramina lifted her brows at Atarah, a humble request in her eyes.

She was beginning to understand Naaman's insistence that his wife needed a helper with a strong voice. She turned to the little one. "Malak," she called out.

He threw a block across the room. Ramina sighed and set her cup aside, then strode over to scoop him up. Gone was the pleasant babe of five minutes before. This little fellow fussed and flailed and rubbed his eyes to make it clear why. Time for his nap, no doubt. Ramina tucked him against her with expert ease and met Atarah's eye again. Her quiet voice had no hope of being heard over Malak's whimpers, but she inclined her head toward another room connected to this one, and Atarah rose to follow her.

A small bed was set up in here, as well as window hangings that diffused the light. Ramina settled Malak onto the bed, humming. He made no attempt to rise again, but he wriggled and whined.

Ramina, a hand on his back, looked to Atarah again. "Naaman's note said that you sing?"

How could her throat feel so dry, when she had just been sipping on nectar? She had sworn to herself she would never open her lips in song. Not for these people.

But these people, despite being Syrians, despite being her captors, were just *people*. An injured mother, a fussy toddler who clearly loved each other. Who looked at her not as a possession but as a friend. Her fingers curled into her palm. "I know only the songs of my people, my lady. The psalms written as praise or supplication to the Most High God."

"Would you sing them to us?"

Not a demand—a request. One that sounded hopeful but perfectly willing to accept a negative answer. Was that possible? Could Ramina really be so kind?

She would have thought herself willing to test it, to try to hold to her silent promise. But just now... Was it such a bad thing, to comfort a little boy? To relieve a mother's distress? To sing to them of the goodness of Yahweh? How could it be? She settled onto her knees beside the little one and could so easily imagine it was one of her siblings. Her fingers stroked over his hair, and she called to her lips the song that had always been the twins' favorite as a lullaby. The fourth psalm.

"You have put gladness in my heart,
More than in the season that their grain and wine increased.
I will both lie down in peace, and sleep;
For You alone, O L*ord*, make me dwell in safety."

Dwell in safety...that should be impossible here, in Damascus, surrounded by people who should be her enemies. Yet the words, as she sang them softly to the boy and watched him settle, worked their way into her heart as well.

God was the Lord of the whole earth, not just Israel. He had worked His miracles in Egypt, in the wilderness, in the Land of Promise before her people had taken possession of it. He was not confined by borders.

He was here. *Yahweh Shammah*. With her. And so, she would abide in Him.

# CHAPTER FIVE

*Two Years Later*

Tavi made one last lunge toward his opponent, slashing down mercilessly with his sword. The man staggered, tripped, and went down with a crash of armor. And a mighty laugh. "Enough!"

The sweat soaking Tavi's own tunic agreed with his mentor's pronouncement. He reached out a hand to help Seena back to his feet. "I think I have finally mastered that thrust."

Seena chuckled as he slapped the dust from his backside. "I should say so. And now that our father has returned with his best horses, we will resume mounted training as well."

Though he had missed the general's warhorses and the hours spent on them each day, the thought of resuming the training right now was enough to make Tavi suck in a long breath. He would never argue—he had not grown so much stronger these two years in Damascus by refusing to push himself—but had he been alone, he might have groaned. He had held nothing in reserve in this morning's maneuvers, and his aching muscles were ready for a respite.

Perhaps Seena heard his mental moaning. He slapped a hand to Tavi's shoulder with another laugh. "I do not mean *now.* Tomorrow. We are out of time today, as well you know. The general will want you with him when he goes to the king. Go." Tavi did not need to be told twice. He dipped his head in respect to Seena and jogged toward the entrance to the barracks, bypassing the other sparring guards still at work in their small enclosure just outside the city gates. Naaman's house was just past the barracks, and if his fellow guards would fall silent for half a moment, he would probably be able to catch a few notes of Atarah's song. She would be on the roof this time of day with Ramina and Malak and little Lilya. His gaze moved that direction, ready to catch any glimpse of them he could.

There—two feminine heads barely visible. Though their hair was almost the same shade, he had no trouble telling which one was Atarah. She stood a few inches taller than the mistress, and her face was tilted toward the heavens. She must be singing.

A momentary break in the sound of clashing practice swords allowed him to catch the briefest hint of melody. Just enough to make his heart brighten.

"I see nothing has changed in the two months I was gone, aside from you learning to best Seena." Naaman stepped out of the shadows of the barracks with a smile, glancing up toward his rooftop as well. "Always with your eyes on the rooftop."

And his master was always quick to tease—and just as quick to keep an eye on the girls himself, whenever possible. "Only because you charged me with their protection, of course."

Naaman barked out a laugh. "Right." He let his gaze linger upward a moment longer before resetting it on Tavi. "How were things in my absence? Truly? I suspect Ramina softened her answers last night when I returned."

And there had been no time before day's end to fill the general in. It had been enough to know he was home from another successful raid. Enough to know that he still lived, and had returned with triumph, to guarantee the king's favor would not be lost.

Tavi let out a long sigh. "Your wife scarcely left the house while you were gone, my lord, so she would not risk crossing paths with Ram or Lebario." He had learned quickly upon his arrival here that Ramina's uncle was every bit as ruthless as his son, and twice as ambitious. "Her aunt visited here several times though. And each time, the mistress needed the calming notes of Atarah's singing afterward as much as Malak once did."

Naaman's right hand fisted. He winced. "Have they not the decency to leave her alone even in her condition?"

Tavi noted the way Naaman dropped his hands. And frowned. He was wearing his leather gloves—not unusual if he was out sparring with the men or working with the horses, but he had been back inside the barracks for half an hour already. Why had he not taken them off? Cooler air had found them, yes, but not so much that he should need gloves for warmth.

As for wondering at the decency of Lebario and his family, that hardly needed to be answered. Ramina's conniving aunt had probably hoped she could cause her some discomfort. Her eyes had held more jealousy than congratulations when Lilya had been born eighteen months ago, and she had not seemed at all pleased to realize a third child would soon join Naaman's family.

Tavi glanced up again, but at the position of the sun this time rather than at the roof. "The king wishes you to join him today, I assume?"

"Yes. We had better clean up."

Tavi followed him into the barracks, frowning at the way the general kept that right arm at his side rather than lifting it in greeting to the guards and menservants he passed. Had he injured it on one of the raids? That would account for the way he was favoring it.

As Tavi headed for water to clean up, he whispered a quiet prayer that whatever wound Naaman hid would be quickly healed.

*My flesh and my heart fail;*
*But God is the strength of my heart and my portion forever.*

Atarah had sung those words just last week, and they had been echoing through Tavi's mind ever since. He knew, with every lift of his practice sword and every lap he ran, that strengthening his body meant nothing if he did not strengthen his heart and spirit as well. If he did not keep El Shaddai at the center of his soul, then the rest would be only vanity.

He washed away the sweat and grime from his morning of exercise, letting every drop of water serve as a reminder of the One who created it. Counting His mercies. Clinging to His promises.

*You have preserved my life, Lord my God. You have preserved Atarah's. You have not only spared us, You have placed us here in a home with good people, people who respect us and care for us. You have surrounded us with other servants who remember You, and together we are free to worship at Your footstool. Your hand has not left us. Your promises are true. Your mercies are new every morning.*

Renewed in mind as well as face, he hurried out to meet Naaman at the front of the house, from which they would make their way into the city. But he frowned as he approached where his master stood, waiting.

He still wore those old leather gloves.

Had anyone else been around, he would have bit his tongue against the question. But they were alone, and so he had no qualms about saying, "My father, I cannot think the king will approve of you wearing those work gloves into the temple of Rimmon."

Naaman looked down at his hands with a clenched jaw and a heavy gaze.

Tavi's stomach felt just as heavy as he stepped near. "General? What is wrong?"

Though it had been five years, he still remembered. He remembered the way Abba had gripped his shoulder in those last moments before the raiders reached them. The way he had looked down into Tavi's eyes and said, "Go. Protect who you can. Call on the Lord. Perhaps He will show you mercy."

He saw the same look in Naaman's eyes now that had been in his father's then. An unnatural calm, shadowed by the sure knowledge that destruction was only seconds away. Tavi could barely force his throat to swallow.

Naaman tugged off the leather from his right hand, revealing the forearm he had kept hidden all morning—and last night too, now that Tavi thought about it. He had kept his cloak draped over his arm the entire evening after his return.

He expected to see a wound, perhaps infected. Something red and angry and ugly.

But it was white that met his gaze. *Too* white. Flaking, peeling, pale skin that made Tavi suck in a quick breath of shock. *Leprosy.* "My father."

Half of him wanted to leap back. Moses had been very clear on how His people were to treat lepers in order to keep everyone around them safe from the disease. It was a *tabu* for a reason.

But things were done differently in Syria. Lepers were not held in the same fear and revulsion. Naaman would not be cast out of the city for this disease eating away at his arm. Not by law, anyway.

He had enemies, though, who would pounce at the slightest sign of a weakness. And this was not slight. It might be but a small patch on his arm *now*, but it would spread.

One thing Tavi knew with complete certainty—he could not possibly abandon this man now. If he meant to protect the rest of the family, Atarah included, it started with protecting Naaman. "When did this appear?"

"Two weeks ago." Naaman fisted his hand, stretched it out again. He did not wince outright this time, but he looked as though he wanted to.

"Did any of your men see it?" Dread curled up in Tavi's chest like an injured beast, ready to strike at any moment. For the most part, Naaman's men were more loyal to him than even to the king.

But there were those who were friends of Ram or associates of Lebario. Who was to say whether they might not sell such useful information?

Naaman shook his head. "We fought against a band of storms most of the way home. When first I noticed it, I thought perhaps it was even just waterlogged from the exposure to the rains. Obviously that was not the case—but my arms were covered all the way home, as were everyone else's. No one has seen. Not even Ramina, thus far."

She would, though. Everyone in the house would, sooner or later.

Later. Right now, their concern had to be the king, who was expecting Naaman to join him at the temple at any moment. And who would be certain to notice those old, worn gloves that had been ragged long before Tavi had first seen them. It was why— He sucked in a breath. "My lord, the new gloves your wife gave you last year! What have you done with them?"

She had taken great pride in the gift, presented some eight months ago. The leather was supple, soft, smooth as olive oil. And she had instructed the craftsman to tool a decorative design into the cuffs. They were so beautiful Naaman had refused to wear them for anything so mundane as training or raiding. They were, he had said, fit only for the grandest of forays.

Naaman's eyes lit. "Of course! Why did I not remember them sooner? Give me two minutes."

He ran into the house, reemerging again quickly enough to prove he had known exactly where he had stored them. And wearing them with a beaming smile that proved they stretched high enough up his arm to cover the damaged flesh.

Tavi nodded his approval. Not that his master needed his approval any more than he needed the paltry protection he could offer as they set off into the city. He was always keenly aware when they entered Damascus that he was but one young man, a foreigner here viewed with suspicion, well trained now but by no means the fiercest warrior on the crowded streets.

Naaman had not begun bringing him along because he really offered any security. No, he suspected his master had him join him so that he could muse to him on the way home. Naaman always left the temple with questions about Ba'al Rimmon and the rest of the gods that other Syrians would have looked at him aghast for.

Questions that gave Tavi leave to speak of a different sort of God. One who loved His people instead of demanding their terror. One who asked for sacrifice not to punish, but to ensure they sought Him and His wisdom first, and to remind them of the very real cost of sin.

Tavi had become more than a pupil and, in turn, confidante than a guard. Which suited him fine, even as it baffled everyone else. It might have baffled Tavi too, if Naaman, when he invited him along, had not looked so much—so oddly—like Elisha had that day in Jezreel.

He would never forget the way the prophet had paused before him. He had been a young man of sixteen, old enough that the recent deaths of his parents had not left him without the ability to see to himself. He had been working in a barley field of a neighbor, had paused for a drink from his water-skin. When he had looked up, Elisha and Gehazi had been standing a few paces away, the prophet's eyes boring holes into him.

In that moment, the strangest thing had crashed over him. A deafening roar in his ears, the din of his own failings. His sins. He had become suddenly aware of all the hatred burning in his heart toward the Syrians, of the brokenness of his spirit. The ugly, burnt crisp of what had once been his heart. He had seen it, felt it, smelled it, heard it, and it left an acrid taste in his mouth and burning down his throat. So horrible that he had dropped to his knees.

He had, for the first time since his parents' death three weeks before, cried. Not with tears, but with a scream from his deepest soul. Bitter, angry noise—but cleansing. When he had risen again, Elisha had clasped him by the shoulders. "I know the place for you," he had said. "If you will follow me to it."

*The place for you.* Tavi had not realized until that moment how much he longed for that very thing. His home had been burned to the ground, and he had no other family in the region. Jezreel had become only the place he lived, where people knew his name. But it had ceased being where he belonged.

He had not gone to ask anyone's permission. He had not looked back at the rows of barley he left unharvested. He merely slung his waterskin over his shoulder and followed Elisha wherever he would lead.

Ramah, that was where they had gone. It had taken endless days of walking, with many stops in towns and villages along the way. Everyone was eager to see the prophet. Everyone was curious about Tavi, the hollowed-out husk of a boy who trailed him. That was all he had been at the time. An empty, broken shell. But when Elisha had finally ushered him into the School of the Sons of the Prophets at Ramah and said this would be his home, the first trickle of life had seeped into the barren landscape of his heart.

By some unfathomable mercy, the Spirit had whispered into Elisha's soul when he had spotted Tavi. By some unfathomable grace, he had been given the chance to learn of the Lord and study His law, as the son of a poor farm laborer should never have had the chance to do. By some unfathomable kindness, the Lord had led him to a place of forgiveness and healing.

And now, by some unfathomable turn of events, it was the favorite general of the Syrian king who looked at him and saw something he should not. Offered chances he should not have. Gave him responsibilities well beyond his rights.

Damascus bustled around them, those who recognized Naaman bowing and scurrying out of the way as Tavi and Naaman strode toward the temple. Those who did not glanced with curiosity at the others' reactions. Soon they approached the place that always made a chill crawl up Tavi's spine—the place where Rimmon supposedly lived.

The king was already waiting, which was enough to make Naaman hiss out a frustrated breath. No doubt all the more frustrated because he was not waiting alone. Lebario, Ram, and a few others were there already too, crowding around Ben-Hadad, weaving a tapestry of flattering words and empty praise.

Praise be to God, the king did not seem to pay them much heed. His eyes lit when he spotted Naaman, and he waved the others away with a sneer that was sure to make their hatred against Tavi's master burn all the hotter. "General!" Ben-Hadad called out as they approached. "I was hoping you were rested enough to join me today in my service to the ba'al. Come. Let me lean upon your arm and you can tell me more of your exploits as we enter."

"Of course, my king." Naaman did not look over his shoulder again at Tavi as they closed the gap.

Tavi's gaze slid over to Lebario and Ram, and that strange feeling came over him. The one he had once thought *only* a feeling, a premonition. The one Elisha had taught him to recognize as something else altogether. A warning, from the Spirit of God to his own.

He eased closer to his master and gave quiet voice to the words that sprang to his tongue. "Beware, my lord, of the vipers ready to sink their teeth into your heel."

It was not safe for Naaman to look back at him. He kept his face toward the king as they mounted the steps. But he whispered back, "I am always expecting that strike, my son. It is why I keep them close—so I can watch them."

"Mm. It is why they stay close too—to watch for their chance." Tavi peeled away at the top of the stairs, heading for the shadows to wait. To watch. To pray.

The dark looks Lebario and Ram exchanged as they followed the king and Naaman into the temple only verified the warning still gripping his stomach.

They would not wait much longer to pounce. And the patch of leprosy on Naaman's arm could well be the opportunity they had been awaiting to destroy him. Naaman would have to take action first.

If only Tavi knew what that action should be.

# CHAPTER SIX

R ain had swept over the land last night along with the returning army, and the cool breeze whispering through the house that afternoon was a welcome change from summer's heat. Atarah danced along with Malak and Lilya as she sang, nearly ruining it with laughter at their sweet movements.

Moses's song spilled from her lips and theirs—the wonders of the Almighty, who had brought His people safely through on dry land and then destroyed Pharaoh's army. They had turned it into a game, this song. She would sing one line, Malak and Lilya the next. Well, mostly Malak. At only a year and a half, little Lilya tried to keep up with her big brother but usually ended squealing and clapping instead of singing a word or two and dancing.

Ramina clapped along too, from her place reclining against the cushions. The sickness had finally left her, and her belly was just beginning to round with the next little one. She moved her lips in time to the words, though her whisper was drowned out by the rest of them.

Atarah whirled Lilya around through the cool air and then landed them both on the pillows with a *whoosh* on the last note of the song. Malak, giggling, jumped on them too. "Another, another!"

Atarah chuckled and tickled him instead. "That was the third song. I need to catch my breath."

In his usual pattern, he took the excuse to curl up next to his mother's side and grinned at Atarah. "Where did you learn all these songs?"

He had asked her the question so many times that it had become part of the game. She grabbed his toes and wiggled them. "From my imma."

He tugged on his foot, though not enough to actually break free. That would ruin the game. "Is she a songbird like you?"

"Oh, no. Not one like me." More familiar words. How many times had she told him of her mother, her family? More than she could count. It felt different today though—probably because last night Naaman had returned from another raid. Today, she had looked out her window and seen the groups still camped outside the walls, given how late they had returned last night, after the city gates had been closed. Today, she remembered what it was like to arrive here as a captive who had no idea what had become of her family.

She settled back against the cushion, letting Lilya scoot onto her lap and settle in. "My imma was a songbird unlike any other in the land. Yahweh Yireh gave her a very special gift, you see. A voice unlike any other's."

"Imma sing?" Lilya blinked big eyes up at her, a finger hooked in her mouth.

Atarah grinned and smoothed the girl's curls down, though they sprang right back up. "That is right, my precious.

My imma sings. When with others, she sings the songs we all do, songs of praise to the Lord of hosts. But her special talent comes when she sings songs of mourning. You see, when we lose someone dear to us, it hurts us in here." She splayed a hand over her own heart and then moved it to Lilya's. "And sometimes, it hurts so much we cannot find words. We do not know how to behave. Sometimes, we try to build walls inside to protect us from the pain."

Lilya's eyes widened. "Need blocks?"

Atarah laughed. "No, sweet one. These walls are not built with your toy blocks. And if we succeed at building those walls, it ends up hurting us more. But my imma—she can break through those walls with her voice. Like...?" She looked to Malak, brows raised.

He bounced in his seat. "Like the walls of Jericho! Crashing down, down, down!"

"Exactly so. The walls inside us come crashing down, down, down when my mother sings. And then the love of the Lord can seep in. We can heal. She can break the hardest hearts with her songs and make a statue cry."

Malak made a face. "No one likes it when *I* cry."

Breathy laughter slipping out, Ramina smoothed the hair back from his forehead. "There is different crying, my sweet. There is the way you cry when your sister has the toy you want, and then there is the way you cry when you fall and skin your knee. One comes from pain, one from anger."

Malak's little brows drew together. "So pain tears are all right?"

"They are. But do you know what is even better? Laughter." Ramina nuzzled his neck with enthusiasm enough to earn shouts of that joyful laughter.

After he had calmed again, Atarah pushed to her feet, Lilya on her hip. She held out a hand toward Malak. "Come, little one. It is nap time."

Malak's lip poked out. "But no! Father will be home soon, and I want to see him!"

"Ah, but the time will pass all the faster if you sleep. When you wake again, he could well have returned from the city." She wiggled her fingers.

He gave a sigh worthy of a grandfather, but he stood and put his small hand into hers. "You will wake me when he returns?"

"Of course." Perhaps not the very minute, but there was no need to say so. With a wink for Ramina, she took the two children into the chamber they shared and tucked them both into their beds, kissed their foreheads, and slipped out again a few minutes later, when both little chests were rising and falling steadily in sleep. She had done a fine job of wearing them out with the songs and dance today.

Her feet took her to the wide window from which she had spotted the camp that morning. They were still there, all the tents and animals and people. And even knowing that Naaman had not gone anywhere near Ramah, she could not help but search the sea of people for some familiar movement. She yearned for it. She dreaded it.

A soft hand touched her shoulder and then retreated. "You are missing your family?"

Atarah drew in a deep breath at the whispered question. "Always. But it is worse when raiders return. I always hope I will see them—and of course, *fear* that I will see them."

"If they were there, my husband would bring them here, at least. You must know that. He would never let anyone else claim your family."

A strange sort of succor. And yet it brought more comfort than she would have thought possible when she first arrived here. Her soul might still cry out for freedom, but she also could not deny that she loved these people. Ramina was like the older sister she had never had. The children like her own siblings, or a niece and nephew. Naaman like a brother or father, who governed his household with care and kindness. If ever anyone else from home were taken captive, she would want them to come here.

But better, of course, was that they remain free.

Assuming they even still lived. She shuddered and rubbed her arms, though it was not the breeze that had cooled her.

Ramina bumped their shoulders together. "They are well. You must believe this. Naaman said the losses in your village were few."

"I know." But *few* still meant *some*. And *some* could have included her parents. Her siblings. "And I am grateful for his mercy." The words that she had scoffed at Tavi for saying that first evening now came so easily to her lips—and she meant every one of them.

Sounds from below drew her closer to the window. She leaned out, peering down. Smiling when Tavi peered up at her from the ground. His lips twitched a bit, eyes smiling where his mouth refused.

"Ah, they are home!" Ramina tugged Atarah back inside. "Come. He will have met with the king in court after they went to the temple."

Which meant that he would have been given his official prize for his successful raid. Gold, silver, spices, animals, slaves—whatever he was given, he called the whole household together to share the honor. And she had quickly learned that he shared it literally, he did not simply gloat over it. They were each given a portion of whatever he had earned, to invest however they willed.

Atarah first checked to make sure the children were still asleep and then followed Ramina down the stairs.

Her gaze flicked to the idol in its dusty display as they passed it, and she wrinkled her nose. Even though the silver statue was ignored by everyone else, she still hated the thing. Were it up to her, she would get rid of it. Or avoid this staircase entirely, so she need not pass by it, at least.

But it was not up to her. Neither the path she could take most of the time nor what became of the idol. And now that Naaman had returned, she knew that instead of cleansing the house from the impurity the ba'al brought into it, they would instead have to clean its nook and polish its figure. The king would come to visit, as he always did in the weeks after a raid, and he would expect to see it well tended.

She trailed Ramina into the main receiving chamber, where Naaman and Tavi and Seena were speaking already. She heard the master instruct Seena to gather everyone together—just as she had expected. It would take a few minutes for everyone to come, though, so she slid over to Tavi's side.

He had grown broader since they came here, more muscled. Occasionally she wondered if her friends at the school would have ever bothered to bat a lash at Abner had Tavi looked then as he did now. Useless to wonder, of course. Her friends, if they had survived the raid, were likely all married by now, with babes in their arms. None of them would ever even see Tavi—see the man he had become or hear him speaking so eloquently with a Syrian general on matters of the soul. She could not be prouder of him, but that pride would have to remain hers alone.

She eased into her usual place at his side and let her fingers tangle with his—it had become a habit during their journey here from Israel, and she had never bothered to break it. He had never chided her for it either, just squeezed her fingers and looked down at her with those smiling blue-green eyes and serious lips. "How was your day?" he asked softly.

"Pleasant, other than seeing the captives outside." He would understand that. "Yours?"

From what she had seen from the rooftop that morning, he had bested Seena in his drills, so he ought to be full of the tale. Perhaps even willing to smile over it. But instead, his lips pressed together and his eyes were troubled.

She squeezed his fingers more tightly. "Tavi? Is something wrong?" She kept her voice at a whisper as low as any of Ramina's.

Tavi glanced over at where the master and mistress were whispering too. Ramina was smiling, stroking a hand over the leather of his gloves.

He had finally worn them. That would certainly account for a bit of the light in her smile. Atarah knew Ramina had not exactly been gratified by her husband calling the gift so precious that he must never dirty them. It had rather defeated the purpose.

Then she realized that Tavi had glanced to Naaman after she had asked if something was wrong, and her music stilled in her chest. All of their fortunes, their very lives, rose and fell with the general's. And they had just come back from meeting with the king.

"What?" she whispered. "What is it? Has he fallen out of favor somehow? Lebario and Ram?"

"No. Nothing like that." Yet even as he said it, he frowned in a way that told her those two had something to do with it.

But not the king, she prayed. "So then?"

He squeezed her fingers again. "He will tell everyone in a few minutes. It is not mine to say beforehand."

She huffed out a breath. Usually it was admirable, Tavi's razor-sharp ideas of right and wrong, honorable and dishonorable. But occasionally it forced her to have far more patience than she really wanted to have. What difference would a few minutes make?

But there was no use in arguing with him. He would insist that the way in which Naaman wanted to share was as important as whatever information he meant to give them.

See? He had presented such logic often enough that she could recite it back to him. Now if only she could take the same comfort in it that he always did.

Other servants began filing in, greeting those already in the room with smiles and soft chatter. There were ten of them who served in the house—maids who handled the cleaning and cooking, menservants who saw to all the heavier matters—and then gardeners and stewards and guards. Naaman had herdsmen too, of course, but they had not yet brought the flocks in for the winter. They ought to be returning any day now.

The room was full a few minutes later, and though Naaman invited everyone to make themselves comfortable, the men all remained standing, leaving the seats to the women. Atarah stayed where she stood at Tavi's side, and no one wasted breath trying to convince her to sit down instead. Not at this point. They just smiled at her and settled in.

Naaman cleared his throat and motioned for quiet. "Thank you all for joining me. I am, as always, grateful for all the work you do to keep this household running smoothly. What rewards I receive, I happily share."

Ramina positively beamed up at him from a step away. "And what favor have you found with the king, my husband? What honor have you won for the house of Naaman?"

It was their usual script, performed without flaw. Naaman launched into a list of what the king had granted him and how much he would give to each of them in turn.

After the first such recitation, Atarah had been completely shocked. A general sharing with his slaves instead of

69

stockpiling all the wealth he possibly could? But today it could not hold her interest—and not because she had long ago realized that Naaman already had more wealth than the whole nation of Israel, it seemed, and would not miss what he gave to them.

No, today she was too distracted by what was wrong to focus on what had gone right. She was too conscious of the way Tavi held himself so stiff and rigid, the way Naaman's eyes seemed darker than usual, dull, as he called each servant forward and put sacks of coins and salt into their hands.

Between the fire in the brazier and the many bodies in the room, it soon grew quite warm, but the master never removed his gloves, even though his cloak came off halfway through the proceedings.

"Tavi." Naaman looked over at them, and a strange something flashed between the two men. "And Atarah too, of course."

They moved forward through the collection of familiar faces.

He handed Tavi his sack first. "For your faithful protection of my family, your eagerness to learn, and your willingness to teach as well, when your master waxes philosophical."

"You do me great honor, my father." Tavi bowed his head.

Then Naaman turned to her and held out a pouch that looked like everyone else's. "And Atarah, for your faithful service to the most precious people in the world—my wife and children. My thanks for bringing music to our souls."

She accepted the jingling bag and dipped her knees. "It is my pleasure, my lord."

They made their way back to their spot, barely able to turn and face him again before he had finished. But rather than dismissing them then as he usually would have done, the general cleared his throat. And looked at Tavi.

Atarah stood as tall as she was able, filled her lungs with air, and summoned an anxious melody to her mind in the hopes that the notes would take her unrest with them and float away.

"There is something else I must tell you all before you return to your tasks." He turned to Ramina. "Forgive me, my love, for not telling you this privately first. I was a coward."

Naaman, a coward? Atarah was not the only one to shift uneasily from one foot to the other.

Ramina, however, betrayed nothing but complete trust. "You are no coward, my husband. If you wish to tell me something with the rest of our household present, I do not begrudge it."

He did not launch into any other speech though. Instead, he tugged at his gloves, pulling off the left one first and then the right.

Then he simply held up his arm. His white, leprous arm.

# CHAPTER SEVEN

A tarah sat at the table with the rest of the servants, but none of them were eating, despite the feast set before them. All the finest foods, prepared for Naaman's victorious return—he always insisted they share the same fare. She wondered if he was having any better luck enjoying it this time than they were.

She picked at the meat, so tender it would likely melt in her mouth, without any desire to taste it. Every time she blinked, she saw that white flesh again. Leprosy. Confined to his forearm right now, but he had said it was spreading. It had been a coin-sized patch two weeks ago and was now the size of her palm. How long before it covered his entire arm? His torso?

Unable to suppress a shudder, she pushed her plate away and looked up at Dafna. None of the Hebrew servants had said a word about it, but they were all surely thinking the same thing—according to the Law of Moses, they were not to be in the same house as a leper. But they hardly had the freedom to observe that law.

The other servants—Phoenicians and Ammonites and other Syrians—whispered only of the consequences of the disease to his health, and so to them all. They had no concerns over uncleanness.

"I cannot think what we will do." Seena, at the head of their table, rested his head in his hand. Distress deepened every line of his face. "The master will seek out the best healers, of course, but there is never any guarantee they will not sell the information of his infirmity to Lebario. No matter how much he may bribe them, everyone in Damascus knows that devil will match it, if it means bringing Naaman low. And what can healers ever do for leprosy?"

"There is surely some treatment we have never heard of." Dafna twisted the end of her shawl around her finger. "There has to be. Perhaps he can find a healer from a foreign land, one who does not know of the rivalry with Lebario. One whose loyalty could be earned or purchased. The patch is still small—he can keep it hidden while he searched out such a man."

"Praise Rimmon that it is the rainy season," another of the guards said. "No one will think anything of it if he keeps his arms covered."

Atarah winced, as she always did at any mention of a ba'al. Two years had not been enough to make her ears accustomed to those names being uttered with blessing instead of cursing. She prayed twenty would not be enough either, or fifty. That her spirit would never overlook the horror of another god's name being invoked.

A soft melody flitted through her mind. One of her mother's songs of mourning. Those were never the songs Atarah chose to sing, but her heart cried them now for her master. For Ramina. For the children. They all deserved better than this.

"No." At Tavi's single word, all noise from around the table stopped. He rarely spoke at meals. Certainly not to disagree with anyone, though he had more than once simply left a room if the conversation turned to idols or other gods. Still, she could hardly believe he was going to argue openly about the mention of Rimmon.

Only, it was not that mention he addressed. He pressed a hand to the worn wood of the table and looked toward Seena, giving Atarah a clear view of his eyes. They blazed in a way she had not seen them do since that first night away from home. As Abba's always had when the Spirit had come upon him. "He must not keep it a secret. I will advise him to tell the king straightaway."

The silence lasted another short, eternal beat. Then a chaos of argument sounded from every corner—from men and women, guards and maids, Hebrews and Gentiles alike.

Atarah just studied this young man she knew better than anyone else in the world at this point—this young man who knew *her* better than anyone else did. He never spoke idly. Rashly. He would never advise anyone, least of all their master, with whom all their futures were tied, to do something he was not convinced was wise. And that light in his eyes said it was not his own wisdom he was relying on just now.

"Tavi?" She did not expect her soft word to even be heard above the continued din. But he looked over at her, and the shift of his gaze must have caught the others' attention. They quieted. "What reason will you give our father for this advice?"

How could eyes the color of water dance with such fire? "The longer he keeps the secret, the worse it will get, and the weaker he will grow. It will be discovered at some point—better to confess it now, when he is still at full strength, when he can combat the enemies who will pounce. Better to get the king on his side at once so that it cannot be presented to him later as a failure and a deception to bring him low in Ben-Hadad's eyes."

This time the silence lasted longer, seeped deeper. The others looked from Tavi to Seena, clearly without a good counterargument.

Seena drew in a long breath then let it out slowly. "You are wise beyond your years, Tavi. When you speak this wisdom to the general, I would be honored to stand at your side and offer my agreement."

Atarah was not about to disagree—not when she knew it was the wisdom of the Almighty Himself spilling from her friend's lips. But even so, she could not imagine how this could possibly go well for Naaman. Perhaps, if he had no enemies ready to devour him…perhaps, if this aging Syrian king could be trusted to remember Naaman's loyalty and honor…perhaps, if she could be certain that Yahweh Rapha wanted Naaman's best, and not to tear down this pillar of the Syrian army that ravaged His people so regularly.

She must be a terrible follower. Surely it could not be godly to wish so fervently that her people's enemy would be delivered of this disease. That he would be healed. That he would remain as he was now—favored and beloved and blessed beyond imagining.

But God saw the heart of man, not just his nationality. Which meant He knew, as everyone in this house did, that Naaman's soul was one who sought all the virtues that the Most High espoused, not the self-serving avarice of the ba'als.

The knot in her stomach would not come undone though. And she could only imagine how much greater would be the one in Ramina's, who ought not to be so harried in her condition. Atarah stood. "The mistress will need me," she whispered by way of an explanation for her departure. Not that anyone so much as looked at her. They were probably all as numbed and worried as she.

As she made for the stairs, she spotted Naaman exiting the house, striding toward the barracks or the stables. Her brows knit, and her pace increased. Her master was always the most conscientious of husbands and fathers. She had assumed he would still be seeking comfort from Ramina—or giving it to her. He had never been the sort to flee in the face of tears.

When she entered the mistress's chambers, however, she heard no crying. The children were playing as usual, though Malak jumped up when he spotted Atarah, clapping his hands together. "Father brought us presents! He is getting them now."

Ah. That explained his absence then, and the purpose of his strides. Atarah dug up a smile for the boy, but it took considerable effort. "Of course he did. How kind of him." She moved to the chaise on which Ramina lounged, searching her mistress's face.

No puffy red eyes greeted her, but her strain was unmistakable—found less in the lines of her face than in the way her fingers dug into the cushion. Atarah settled to a seat on the floor beside her. "Are you all right, my lady?"

Ramina kept her eyes on the children and blinked far too quickly, far too many times. "My husband will get through this. Somehow. He will not be one of throngs of lepers begging in the streets."

"Of course not." That was an image that would not even solidify in her mind. She reached up to cover Ramina's tense fingers with her own. "We will get through this."

Ramina's lips quavered. "How?" The word, fainter even than usual, was more a tremor than a sound. She cleared her throat and averted her face from the children, no doubt to hide the tears that had welled in her eyes despite all that blinking. "Were my mother alive, she would be saying that we must beseech Rimmon. That it has been my dishonoring of the ba'al that has led to this and that we must make amends."

"No." Atarah squeezed her mistress's fingers. "Ba'al is not the answer."

She did not seem to hear her. Her free hand had splayed across the gentle rounding of her belly. "She would say this child would have to be sacrificed to him. To appease him."

"No!" Atarah regretted the volume of her rebuke the moment the word screeched from her lips, but praise the Almighty, the children laughed about something at that very moment and paid her no heed. Still, she leaned closer to Ramina and lowered her voice. "My lady, you know as well as I that Rimmon is not a god who heals. You must not even consider such a thing. It was the blood crying out from the land that led Yahweh to take Canaan from the other nations to begin with and give it to my ancestors. Life is sacred to Him. Precious. It must not be spilled to other gods."

Ramina sat up, leaned over to touch her forehead to Atarah's. "I know. I do. I would never... But my sister, what are we to do? Rimmon does not heal, but your Yahweh Yireh will surely not either, not for us. We are not His people. He is not our God."

"He was not Ruth's God either, not originally. But she chose to believe, to follow, and became the great-grandmother of our greatest king. Yahweh is the God who sees, my lady—He sees our hearts."

"Then He sees mine breaking today." Ramina pulled back and dashed away the tears wetting her cheeks. "Naaman deserves better than this. Leprosy! Does even your God heal this?"

"Of course He does. Remember? He healed Miriam of leprosy."

Something flickered across Ramina's face. Not quite hope but its shadow, anyway. "I had forgotten."

Because Miriam's song, which Atarah had sung for them many times, spoke only of the victory over the army of Pharaoh. But the God who parted the Red Sea and allowed the people of Israel to cross on dry land was the same God who held healing in His hand.

And Atarah needed to remember that. Yahweh was God over everything—even this. She drew to her mind the words of one of the psalms that spoke of healing. The thirtieth. "May I sing for you?"

A smile fluttered over Ramina's lips. "Please."

As she sang, she silently thanked the Lord for bringing this particular song to mind. It started with just the words her mistress would need:

"I will extol You, O LORD, for You have lifted me up, and have not let my foes rejoice over me. O LORD my God, I cried out to You, and You healed me."

And then it ended with the promise they all must cling to—that He would turn their mourning into dancing.

By the time she finished the song, the children were indeed dancing, Malak spinning little Lilya around with a bit too much exuberance. But she squealed with laughter and managed not to fall. And what was more, Ramina's face had brightened a few degrees.

Atarah drew a deep breath in when she had finished, another truth settling on her spirit like the kiss of lamplight. "Mistress... there is a prophet in Israel. He could heal your husband."

"Elisha?" Ramina's whisper held a note of awe—the same one that had no doubt saturated Atarah's tone every time she told her of him and of Elijah before him. "He *could*—but would he?"

That she did not dare to promise. How could she, a mere daughter of one of Elisha's men, promise anything on his behalf? Who was she to understand the workings of God to that extent? But she recalled the flame of the Spirit in Tavi's eyes just a few minutes ago.

Why would God send His Spirit, His truth, to Tavi if they were not meant to use it? Atarah wet her lips as she weighed her words. "I believe he would, if the master sought him with the right heart."

Ramina sprang to her feet with more energy than she had displayed in weeks, rushing for the door. Atarah barely managed to stand before she realized that Naaman had come back up, his arms full of wrapped parcels that must be the gifts for the children.

But his wife paid no attention to them. She gripped Naaman's arms, her whispers feverish. Atarah could not hear her exact words over the children, but she did not need to hear them. She knew what she would be saying, and Naaman's startled gaze flying to her verified it.

He shook his head, storm clouds in his eyes.

Atarah's heart sank.

Malak and Lilya spotted their father and darted over to him, bouncing and clapping.

With a long sigh, Atarah eased back down to a seat, on the chaise this time. She watched as he presented them with their gifts, but she could not have said what he gave them. What did it matter? They were just things—things that would do nothing to heal their father. To save their futures. To preserve their family.

A few minutes later, the little ones were happily engrossed with those useless *things*, and Ramina was tugging Naaman toward Atarah, her hoarse whisper the closest thing to outright begging that Atarah had ever heard from her.

"Please, my love. Let her tell you about this prophet. If Elisha could heal you—"

"It is out of the question." Yet Naaman did not sound harsh when he said it, merely resigned. He watched his children, his good arm around Ramina's shoulders. "I am the right hand of Ben-Hadad, my sweet one, who is an avid devotee of Rimmon. I cannot go and seek healing from some other God, some other prophet. The king will take it as a personal slight."

"So what, then? Will you seek healing from Rimmon?" Ramina touched a hand to the scar on her throat. And then let it fall to her stomach.

Naaman's head bowed. "You know I will not. That I would never consider sacrificing our babe, no matter what god demanded it."

He darted a gaze toward Atarah, and she stiffened. Usually when Naaman was in the room she chose silence, unless she was invited to sing or otherwise participate in the conversation. She felt no particular fear of him—he had proven himself over and again to be a good man, a kind master. But that meant he deserved respect, the same sort she would give her own father.

At this inference, though, she found words springing unbidden to her lips. "Yahweh would never ask such a thing. He proved it by providing a ram for Abraham in order to spare his beloved son."

He could have rebuked her for butting into the conversation. Instead, he sent her a tired, sorrowful smile. "I appreciate your heart, Atarah. And that you would recommend your own prophet as a possible healer. But I am no Israelite."

She really ought to bite her tongue and leave it at that, to focus her efforts on convincing Ramina and let *her* be the one to convince Naaman. If only she could make her mouth obey. "Yahweh is not the God of only the Israelites, my lord. He is God of all, Creator of heaven and earth. He called Abraham out from among the nations. He gave dreams to Pharaoh. He called many Egyptians out with the Hebrews when He led us to the Promised Land. He is the God Who Sees."

She had his attention, whether it was wise of her to seek it or not. So she prayed the Lord would help her use it wisely. She splayed a hand over her chest. "He sees me, a slave girl in a foreign land. He sees Tavi, who is without mother or father, who has neither an acre nor a coin to his name beyond those you have given him. Why would He not see *you*, a general who commands respect and deserves it? A man who has the ear of the king?"

Ramina wrapped her arms around her husband's torso. "When Miriam, sister of Moses, was struck with leprosy, it was for a purpose. Because she had questioned the Lord. But it was also an opportunity—a chance for the God of Israel to show Himself capable. He healed her. He could heal you, Naaman. I know He could. To show Himself great in Aram-Damascus."

Atarah's throat felt as tight as Ramina's always sounded. She had grown up among the very descendants of Abraham— in arguably one of the most devout communities in all the nation, where idols were not tolerated and the Law was taught morning, noon, and night. But even so, she had rarely heard faith proclaimed so simply, so surely. That God could do the impossible. God could heal.

"Please, my lord. My father." Though others called him that frequently—Tavi included—she never had. She *had* a father, and he was a prophet of the Most High, not a general in Syria. But somehow she suspected Abba would understand the need to appeal to Naaman from the heart. "Consider it—that is all we ask. Consider seeking out Elisha for healing."

The silence pulsed long and tense, somehow all the more apparent because of the oblivious chatter of the children. After an eternal moment, he blustered out a breath. "I will consider it. That is all I can promise."

For today, it would have to be enough.

# CHAPTER EIGHT

Tavi trailed Naaman through the city, following a few steps behind him, as usual. Seena was a few steps ahead, parting the crowds for the general. Tavi found it encouraging that, of all the guards he could have called on, Naaman had chosen them to accompany him on this trip to the palace today. He and Seena were the only two of all the menservants to insist over and again that he must tell the king about the leprosy.

He had not told them why he sought the king today—but their very presence surely meant he was heeding their advice. Did it not?

Tavi hoped so—prayed so. Never in his life had he spent so many hours in prayer each day, beseeching the Most High on Naaman's behalf. Perhaps God would heal him outright, through some quiet miracle worked in his own house. Perhaps He would see fit to use him or Atarah or Dafna or one of the other Israelites to accomplish it.

Perhaps…but he suspected not. The more he prayed, the more convinced he was that in order to be healed, *Naaman* must take action. He must take a step of faith. Embrace Yahweh for himself, not just allow them to worship Him. And thus far, Naaman had not made any indication he would do that.

Until today, he had not even made any indication that he would tell the king about the leprosy.

They passed the temple of Rimmon, a glowering hulk of a building that he was happy to skirt around today. The streets beyond were not nearly so familiar to him as those leading to it. Only rarely had Naaman taken him on an errand to the palace itself—usually he chose the older of his guards for such trips, those decorated in war and well known throughout the city as accomplished warriors. A show of force, meant to declare Naaman's power.

And to dissuade certain parties from attempting anything so foolish as an assassination cloaked as a street robbery.

Tavi listened with half an ear to the merchants hawking their wares in the marketplace. Dozens of voices danced in a sort of music all their own, the notes a steady rise and fall and the lyrics naming every staple and luxury the world had to offer. Dates and figs and oranges, saffron and cinnamon and salt, leather and papyrus and dye.

Naaman paused briefly at a goldsmith's workshop, apparently to check on something he had commissioned for Ramina. Tavi lingered near the entrance of the shop while the smith showed the general what progress he had made on…a necklace, it looked like. One of the large, wide ones that would cover most of the mistress's chest. She had a few other such pieces, only ever worn when they entertained or attended a gathering at someone else's home, which was rare.

Tavi's gaze went to a few bangles set out for display. Atarah used to wear bracelets like those on feast days in Ramah. Hers had been only bronze, perhaps with a bit of silver. Nothing so fine as these. But he had always liked the way they jangled together when she sang, given the way she raised her arms, clapped, swayed. They were like wrist tambourines, Abner had joked once.

She should have a new set of them. Not from here, of course—even with Naaman's generosity to them all, Tavi did not have coins to spare on gold bangles. But he could get her silver ones, perhaps. If he could bargain with a silversmith well enough. And the flash of silver would contrast beautifully with the bronze of her skin.

Seena's chuckle interrupted his thoughts. His mentor slid up beside him. "Dreaming of gifts for your lady?"

Would he believe him if Tavi claimed he only wanted to get her an instrument for her singing? To make her a better servant to Ramina?

No, he was not so stupid. Tavi only shrugged.

Seena elbowed him in the side. "When will you speak to the master about her? Hmm? You are both of age. And anyone with eyes can see how smitten you are."

Tavi glanced over his shoulder, though there was no one else in the shop to overhear them. How to explain that Naaman's was not the blessing he wanted in this particular case? He could not—Seena would only remind him that he was Naaman's slave. He was not free to seek anything from Atarah's father anymore. It was enough to say, "Now is not the time. Not with...everything else."

His friend sighed. "I suppose you are right about that. Though it would be nice to have something to celebrate."

"We will celebrate our father's victory over his enemies. And, Lord willing, his healing." If only Atarah and the mistress could convince him to seek out Elisha. As soon as Tavi had heard that they had recommended it, his spirit had quickened. *Elisha, yes. Elisha could heal Naaman. If he would go to him.*

Seena opened his mouth, but before he could reply, Naaman rejoined them, assuring the goldsmith that he found the work most pleasing thus far and looked forward to seeing the completed piece soon.

A moment later, they were on the streets again. And soon after that, the walls of the palace loomed above them.

Though Tavi had only been here twice in his two years in Damascus, Naaman was a well-known figure, and the guards admitted him with respectful bows. Seena fell behind him now, he and Tavi walking with matched strides, matched uniforms, matched movements. Perhaps that was why Naaman had brought him today, now that he paused to consider it. With all the sparring they had been doing, he and Seena were more alike in their mannerisms and posture than the other guards were. And he was the only one of them the same height as their trainer. There were others taller, several shorter. But his build had grown to be quite similar to Seena's these last two years.

He glanced at his friend from the corner of his eye as they climbed the stairs. Had his father been his size? His memories had faded too much for him to recall. Abba, in his mind, was enormous—as he had seemed when Tavi was a lad not yet come into his own height, and certainly not into his breadth. He had seemed like a strong tower, a fortress to him then.

But the Syrian soldiers had cut him down as if he were no more than a stalk of wheat—his plowshare no match for their swords and spears. He must have been, in reality, of only average height. Probably similar to how tall Tavi now stood.

A moment more and the winter sunlight gave way to the dim interior of the palace, punctuated by sconces on the walls, burning precious oil even in the daytime. Their footfalls echoed through the stone corridor, only partially muffled by the rich tapestries adorning the walls. At the end of the hallway, two massive doors were opened at their approach, revealing the throne room within.

Ben-Hadad, king of Aram-Damascus, sat on his throne with a rather bored look on his face. He wore his gray hair loose today, a circlet of gold around his head anchoring it in place. It was apparently not a day for hearing the appeals of the citizens, given how few people were in the room. There were perhaps a dozen court officials about their business, and otherwise only the guards and cupbearers and other servants to be seen.

A few more steps revealed that the men sitting near the king, seemingly boring him to tears, were none other than Lebario and Ram. Of course.

Tavi heard Seena's hiss of disapproval, though no one else was near enough to do so. He barely refrained from grunting in response. Those two never missed an opportunity to spread on a new layer of flattery, to ingratiate themselves. Nor did they ever miss a chance to glare at Naaman, as they did now at his approach. From what Tavi had been able to glean, their family had long been close to the king's, and more than once Lebario had offered Ben-Hadad wise counsel that had helped Aram-Damascus grow. According to Naaman, there had even been a time when he and his rival had been friends. Over the years, however, jealousy had crept in. Perhaps Lebario's advice to the king was still generally sound, but success had darkened his soul with greed.

The general bowed before the king, holding the position until Ben-Hadad said, "General Naaman! Excellent. Come, sit. You are just the man to weigh in on Lebario's suggestion that we consider an alliance with Irhuleni of Hamath."

Naaman straightened and moved to the vacant chair on the king's other side. Tavi and Seena shadowed him, taking up their positions behind him. It gave them a fine view not only of the court but of Lebario and Ram.

They smiled, both of them. Matching turns of matching lips. But Tavi could have sworn he saw a snake's tongue flash from Lebario's mouth as he said something about the wisdom of an alliance.

Tavi blinked, knowing it must have been his imagination. Still, his eyes did not clear. He saw Lebario's too-familiar face shift in its shape, the wrinkles smooth out and turn to scales, his eyes turn slitted. And that viper tongue, forked and testing, flicked out again.

*Lord?* He gripped the spear, which had become an extension of his arm through his months of training, to steady himself. He had heard of visions from Yahweh, of course. Everyone at the school had. But he had never received one. Was this an image from God or just his own fears and suspicions taking visual form? Whichever it was, he silently prayed for wisdom for himself, for Seena, and for Naaman. For strength. For courage.

For the next ten minutes, Naaman simply talked of politics as he likely always did when here, making Tavi glad he was rarely invited along. But then he noted a change in his master's demeanor. It started as a wince when he motioned with his hand, which must have made the leather of his glove chafe against the flesh beneath it. The wince turned to a stiff shoulder, a spine straighter than usual, and breathing so even that he was clearly making an effort to keep it regulated.

"My lord, I was hoping I might be granted a moment of your attention for another matter, when it is convenient for you," Naaman said when there was a lull in the conversation.

Ben-Hadad perked up a bit. "Of course! You know you may speak of anything you like, any time."

"I thank you for that." Naaman made a show of lowering his head. Then he darted a glance toward his wife's uncle and cousin. "I daresay this is of no interest to anyone else, though. It can wait for a private audience. Perhaps you would grant us the pleasure of hosting you for dinner one day soon?"

The king always dined with them within a fortnight of Naaman's return from the field, so it was certainly not an odd invitation.

But Ben-Hadad waved a hand. "Yes, you know I will. Name the day. But do not think you can pique my interest and then demur, my friend." He chuckled. "What other matter do you wish to bring up that has your shoulders so tight?"

Ah, so the king was not as bored behind those half-lidded eyes as he had seemed. Tavi's respect for him rose a notch.

"Do not let our presence deter you." Ram offered a snake smile. "Anything of interest to my beloved cousin's husband is naturally of interest to us as well."

*Wisdom. Strength. Courage. Please, Yahweh, fill him with these things. Guide him.*

Naaman was still for a long moment, making Tavi wish he could see his face and try to read his decisions in his eyes. But apparently the quirk of Ben-Hadad's brow was sufficient prompting. Naaman reached for his glove, tugged it off, and held up his arm. "I do not wish to hide anything from you, my father."

The king leaned a little closer, squinting. "What is it? An injury? No—a dry patch?"

"A small patch of leprosy, my lord." Naaman's voice did not shake, did not rise. He sounded perfectly calm, unalarmed— the same voice he had used when telling his own household about it, the one that insisted that all was under control without any need for exaggerated assurances.

"Hmm." The king sat back again, though slowly enough to prove it caused him no great distress. "A very small patch—it can surely be tended. I will send my personal healer to take a look at it today."

"I will receive him with gratitude. Though I have already had my own healer tend it."

And had paid him a ridiculous sum to guarantee he would not breathe a word of it to anyone outside the household, though of course Naaman would not mention that here.

"And? What were his thoughts?" Ben-Hadad no doubt knew that Bareil, Naaman's preferred healer, was just as talented as the king's.

Naaman cleared his throat. "He offered some advice on salves and scraped off the dead skin. It seems that otherwise he advises waiting and seeing if it spreads."

Ben-Hadad made a face. "*Waiting* has never been my preferred course of action. Though you are a man of more patience than I."

Naaman breathed a laugh. "I confess I am lacking in it this time."

"Well, if there is anything else that can be done, do it. I will not have my best general compromised by any ailment that can be helped. Surely there is a spring you can bathe in or a treatment of some foreign salt that would heal it. We will seek out any answers to be found. And offer a bull to Rimmon on your behalf."

"Of course." Naaman's voice was as even as ever, though Tavi's fingers tightened again around the shaft of his spear. He would just as soon no attention ever be brought on Naaman before the idol and whatever demon he represented. "Although…"

Tavi went still. Although?

The king leaned forward again. "Although? Although what?"

Naaman sighed and averted his face. "It is probably nothing. But my wife's handmaiden—she mentioned that there is a prophet in Israel who could heal me."

The king lifted his brows.

Lebario and Ram laughed outright, the elder slapping his son on the shoulder. "The Hebrew God—Lord of lepers! That sounds about right!"

"Lebario, really." The king looked half-offended, half-amused. "One spot of leprosy does not a leper make. Or at least you ought to hope such, otherwise your own small infirmities may become the thing for which you are known."

Dark light flashed through Lebario's eyes. "Forgive me, my lord. I meant no disrespect to my esteemed nephew. It was the invisible Hebrew God I cannot respect."

"Even so. One cannot discount all the history that tells the tales of their God's power." He turned to Naaman again, giving Tavi an unrestricted view of his face. His expression was thoughtful, serious. "Perhaps you ought to seek out this prophet. If he can heal you, then so be it. If not, you are no worse off than you are now."

Some of the tension in Naaman's shoulders eased. "If you will it, my lord and king."

"I do." He clapped and waved a hand at one of the servants. A scribe, it seemed, given that the man scurried over with a writing tablet and stylus. "I will send a letter of introduction for you to King Joram of Israel. And you must take an adequate entourage, so he knows to take you seriously. Choose a hundred of your own men to accompany you."

Ram eased forward. "I would be honored to be counted among that number, my lord."

If Tavi squeezed the spear's shaft any tighter, it would either snap or meld permanently to his hand. Ram had not gone on Naaman's last expedition, and they had all breathed a sigh of relief over it. Their household all believed he asked for these assignments solely to sow discontent among Naaman's men and look for any available means to undermine him. According to Atarah, Ramina even feared he might turn on Naaman in the heat of battle one day and kill him outright, if he thought he could do so without being seen.

"Excellent," the king replied. "Ninety-nine more, then. And your own guards, of course." Ben-Hadad actually glanced past Naaman to Tavi and Seena, bestowing a royal nod upon them. "Your man does train the best, I know. Who is this young fellow? He looks strapping."

Tavi's ears burned. He would have been quite happy to have never actually had the Syrian king's gaze resting upon him.

Naaman chuckled. "His name is Tavi—he too is a Hebrew. Have you not noticed him before, my lord? He accompanies me to the temple nearly every day."

"Does he?" The king did not seem to mind his own lack of observation. "I suppose he does not draw the eye so much when he is not standing like a mirror image of Seena. I thought none could ever match him."

Had it been another of Naaman's servants making the observation, Tavi would have been quick to assure them that he was no true match for Seena, not really. He still had much to learn at his mentor's hand. But he did not dare speak to the king unless asked a direct question, so he kept his gaze straight ahead, as expected.

"Seena has taken a special interest in him," Naaman said. "He is quite proud of all he has accomplished, and rightfully so. A good pupil and a good teacher make for a pair I am grateful to have guarding my household."

Tavi let his breath ease out. *This* was why Lebario and Ram had utterly failed at ousting Naaman from the king's favor. There was no man in all the world so capable of putting honor where it rightfully belonged. Which meant, without ever claiming any for himself outright, he received more than anyone. Deservedly so.

The king turned his attention to the scribe, much to Tavi's relief. He could hardly wait to get home—Atarah would be thrilled to learn that Naaman was taking her advice. He would seek out Elisha.

And if God saw fit to answer the new prayer that sprang to life in Tavi's spirit, perhaps that meant he would have the chance to see his homeland and the prophet once more.

# CHAPTER NINE

The entire house was a flurry of activity—from the kitchen staff who were busy preparing food enough for the journey to the guards drilling for the chance to be included in the number going with Naaman.

Atarah watched them from the rooftop, her gaze always finding Tavi within moments. Though some of the older guards could still outdo him in some skills, she knew that in general strength and grace, he was a match to any of them.

Which made her heart sink like a stone in her chest. He deserved the honor of traveling with Naaman—but selfishly, she hoped he was instead assigned the task of guarding them here at home. Naaman had already said he would be leaving half of his best here for that purpose. *Let it be Tavi's half,* she silently pleaded. *Please, Lord.*

It was only partly selfish, really. She would miss him dreadfully if he was gone, yes. He was her dearest friend, the only one who really knew her for all she was. But it was more than that. She *trusted* him, with her own life and Ramina's and the children's.

And given the way Ramina's aunt had been measuring every room in the house as if picking out new tapestries for the walls that afternoon, it was no wonder the mistress was quieter than usual as she sat against the low wall of the roof, watching the drills as well.

"Do not look so forlorn, my love. I am going to see a prophet, not to war."

Atarah jumped at the voice, turning to see Naaman at the top of the stairs, Malak riding on his shoulders. Lilya had not yet awakened from her afternoon nap.

Ramina turned to her husband with pleading eyes. "I have made a decision, my husband. We will all accompany you—me, the children, all the servants who are not required here."

Naaman just stared at her.

Atarah stared at her too. Her mistress had not breathed a word of this idea in all the fortnight since the plan had been set in motion for Naaman to journey to Samaria. How long had she been considering it? And was this dread or joy beating so heavily in her own chest?

She wanted more than anything to return to Israel. And yet she did not want to return to Israel as a slave.

Then her own concerns fled. Her master still said nothing, so Atarah pointed out the obvious in his stead. "Mistress, you are in no condition for such a long journey. You must think of the babe."

"I *am* thinking of the babe." She rested her hand on her stomach but did not take her eyes from her husband's face. "Do not leave me here, my love. Not this time. Something has changed with my aunt and uncle—I do not know what, but I fear it. They have some plan, I know they do. I could see it in her eyes today when she came to visit. She was all but crowing with it."

"Ramina. My sweet one." Naaman lowered Malak to the ground and moved to sit beside Ramina. He took her hand in his. "You have nothing to fear. They can do nothing to us."

"Can they not?" Ramina shook her head. "My cousin could kill you in your sleep while you are away and claim it was the curse of the Hebrew God—or of Rimmon, because you sought another deity. And Lebario could then kill me, all of us, claiming you had brought a curse on the whole family and he had to halt it before it spread to him. No one would question him. Not if you were not here."

It was a valid enough fear to make Naaman frown, which in turn made Atarah's breath catch. A wisp of melody floated through her mind, and she hummed it without pausing to think about it.

Until Ramina and Naaman both looked over at her with matching wary expressions.

She realized only then that it was the familiar strains of Moses's song she had hummed. The one that sang of the might of the Lord and of how He dashed His enemies to pieces. A victorious song, one she had always loved.

But she had always been singing it as a child of Abraham, one of God's chosen. Never had she paused to think of how it would sound to Gentile ears.

Naaman drew in a long breath. "I know the enemies I have here at home, waiting to pounce. But tell me truly, Atarah—what enemy do I have in your Most High? Do I really dare go before Him and ask of Him a favor?"

She wanted to assure him that it was the best possible choice, the only real course of action. But a dozen stories filtered into her mind, many of which she had either sung or told to Ramina and the children. Of Pharaoh's army, yes. Of Jericho. Of Aaron's sons, who fell down dead when they did not follow the details of the Lord's instruction. Of the fifty thousand men killed for looking into the ark when the Philistines returned it to the Land. Of the plague that struck seventy thousand because King David had taken a census.

The Lord was a jealous God, a meticulous God. A God who saw heart and actions both. A God who was holy and insisted His people be so too.

And yet He was the Savior of those who called on Him. "Yahweh is not a tame God, my lord. He is not a lifeless idol. He is Fire, and He is Light. He is Perfect Truth—but He is also Perfect Love. If you seek Him with reverence, then He is not your enemy. But know that He is the God Who Sees. He will see your heart in perfect clarity. He will know if any unrighteousness dwells in you."

Naaman leaned back and raked a hand through his silver-threaded hair. "What hope have I, then? I am no Jew. I do not even *know* your Law, so I certainly do not follow it. But is this not what determines righteousness in your God's eyes?"

Even as she nodded, she frowned. Her abba had taught them all the Law, to be sure. But especially when they were little, he had taught them first and foremost this. "The heart of the Law, my father, is very easily summed up. To love the Lord our God

99

with all our hearts, with all our souls, with all our minds, and with all our strength. And to love others as we love ourselves."

"How do I love Him so fully, when all I know of Him is what you and Tavi and Dafna and the rest have shown me?" Naaman rubbed his neck. "Of all the gods I know of, He seems...different from the rest. He is the only one who draws such attention to holiness and uprightness of spirit. This appeals to me, but... who am I? Who am I to approach Him?"

"The best man I know. Who has a heart always seeking goodness and truth—the very things their Elohim stands for." Ramina took his hand—the gloved one, that had been sitting idly in his lap. She raised it to her lips and pressed a kiss to the leather. "If you die, my husband, I die with you. You know this will be so, whether we choose it or not. And so, if we die, then let it be at the hand of their righteous God rather than my selfish uncle."

Malak had been playing with the marbles he had left up here earlier in the day, but at this he came over and crawled between his parents, wrapping his little arms around them both. "We will not die, Mother. God protects us." He turned wide eyes on Naaman. "We go with you to meet Him, Father? Please? I will be very good. No complaining. Promise. And Lilya." He made a face. "No promises for Lilya."

Naaman chuckled and kissed his son's cheek. "I know you would both be wonderful companions for the journey." He looked over his head, to Ramina. "Are you certain about this? I cannot think your lot is firmly entwined with my own. Even if the worst were to happen to me, that does not mean—"

"We both know it does." Ramina tilted her head back, giving them all a clear view of the vicious scar. "Were it not for you, my cousin would have killed me that night. And he has never forgiven you for stopping him. My uncle already hated you for being more successful. When we chose each other, we fortified them as our mutual enemies."

Naaman squeezed his eyes shut. "All I ever wanted was to protect you. Provide for you. To think that you could suffer because of me—"

"I would rather suffer for you than live like a queen for anyone else." She leaned over and placed a kiss just beside his mouth. "Please, my husband. Let us come."

Atarah tangled her fingers through the scarf that had fallen to her shoulders, holding her breath.

At last, Naaman heaved a great sigh and nodded. "Very well. We are Yahweh's to deal with as He wills. Atarah—go tell the others, if you would. Everyone but the few required to tend the house in our absence will go with us."

She did not need to be told twice. She flew down the stairs and into the house proper, shouting the news to the other servants as she passed them, not pausing to give any more than the basic information to Dafna and the steward. Then she was moving again, hurtling out the door, headed for the courtyard where the guards were still drilling.

"Tavi! Seena!" She flew toward them, heedless of the other guards sparring around her. Though they all stopped as she sped past, probably wondering what sort of emergency she brought news of.

Tavi dropped his dull-edged sword as she approached, meeting her halfway and gripping her arms. "What? What is it?"

For a moment she just stared into his eyes, blue as the sky and green as the grass. *Home.* If only briefly, they were going home. "The master has said we are *all* going. All of us."

"Truly?" Seena had come up too, frowning. "Is that not dangerous, with the mistress in her condition? If something happens to us on the journey, the entire household would be wiped out. His name possibly gone forever."

"The mistress insisted that it is better to die with him than without him."

Seena obviously did not need it spelled out any more than that. Lips in a thin line, he nodded. "She has a point. I know I would rather fall at his side than be stabbed in the back by one of Lebario's men. So be it." He spun to the rest of the men. "Good news! You have all been chosen to accompany our lord!"

A mighty roar went up, as if they had each been given the greatest honor rather than the contest being canceled. Atarah smiled—and made no complaint when Tavi tugged her out of the little arena and toward the shelter of the wall. "I did not realize the mistress wanted to go."

"Neither did I." She rearranged the thin scarf, mostly to keep her hair out of her face. "She asked him moments ago, and it was the first I had heard of it. She is genuinely frightened of what Lebario could do to them if something happens to the master though. And by 'happens,' I mean…"

"I know." Tavi looked out over the courtyard, at where his comrades darted this way and that, gathering things they might need on the journey. "I think this is a wise choice. And a blessing for us. We will get to see Israel again."

"I know." The wonder of it brought her voice down to a whisper. "I know we will go first to Samaria to present ourselves to the king—but Elisha may not be there this time of year. He could be anywhere. Mount Carmel. Jezreel. Ramah."

*Ramah.* She had to squeeze her eyes shut. Maybe he and Gehazi would be in her hometown. Maybe they would be at the School of the Sons of the Prophets. Maybe Naaman would seek him there, all of them with him, and walk right up to the school.

Maybe she would finally know what had become of Abba and Imma. Of her brothers and sisters. Of her friends. Perhaps she would learn whether Joshua had come home to marry Sahar yet. Whether she had a niece or nephew that she ought to add to her prayers.

Her eyes sprang open again. She too looked out at the movements of the guards, but she saw only a blur. "How will we do it, Tavi? How will we go home and then leave it again?"

"Will you try to convince me to run away again?"

At the teasing note in his voice, she angled her face up. And was blessed with one of his rare smiles, bright and full. It made music burst to life in her heart. She grinned back. "Then who would teach the new babe about Yahweh? No. You were right, that the Lord put us here. Perhaps…perhaps for this. So that we could lead our master to the Most High. To his healing."

"Perhaps so."

"Only…it would be so nice to know. Whether they survived the raid."

"God willing, we will have the chance to ask Elisha or Gehazi while we are there. They would know."

They would. Of course they would. Whether they ended up in Ramah or met Elisha directly across the border, he would certainly have that information. So if all she truly desired was the knowledge, then she was sure to find it.

The fact that her heart did not entirely quiet told her it was not *all* she desired. She wanted to embrace her imma. To spend another evening listening to her abba's stories. To braid Channah's hair and listen to Havah boast about how she could out-sling their brothers.

But those desires were unlikely to be met, and she would have to accept that. She laced her fingers through Tavi's. Without his constant presence, his constant reminders to keep her eyes on Yahweh Shammah, she might never had thought to recommend that Naaman seek Elisha. "Could you do something for me?"

"Anything." He said it so quickly, without any hesitation.

She smiled up at him. "Remind me whenever necessary that this journey is not about us. It is not about going home. It is about Naaman and Ramina and their children. It is about his healing and their survival. It is about the chance for them to see firsthand the might and power of El Shaddai."

A true miracle happened—Tavi smiled for the second time in five minutes, an event she could never remember seeing before. He leaned over and kissed her on the top of the head. "I am proud to be your friend, Atarah."

A new line of melody joined the song still singing through her from his first smile. "You cannot be half so proud as I am of you. All you have accomplished, all you have learned—and yet still you seek God first and last. I do nothing but sing and tend the children."

"Nothing but?" He laughed—actually laughed! "Atarah, you have taught the entire household of God through those songs. You are more a teacher of His ways than any at the school."

Well. She would never claim *that*. But she was not going to argue with him.

She could not imagine ever doing anything to interrupt that beautiful laughter. It was far sweeter than any music she had ever heard, on harp, lyre, or timbrel.

# CHAPTER TEN

Samaria, the capital of Israel, lay just ahead of them. The sun was still at its zenith, shining gold on the stones of the walls, and Atarah soaked in the sight of it with a smile. She had never had cause to travel here with her family—only her father had ever traveled more than twenty miles from home. Who would ever have guessed that she would come here with a Syrian general, of all people?

"Look!" Malak tugged on her hand, hopping up and down as he pointed at...a flock of sheep? What was so interesting about that? "A shepherd! Is it David?"

She laughed and tousled his hair. "No, Malak. I am afraid David was a shepherd boy many, many years ago. He has since grown up, become king, and died. One of his descendants rules Judah in Jerusalem—the king in Israel now is Joram."

Malak's face fell. Apparently he had been quite looking forward to meeting the shepherd king who wrote many of his favorite songs. Atarah looked up to exchange a grin with Ramina. Their journey had been made as easy on her as possible, with a luxurious wagon at her disposal for whenever she grew tired. Even so, she had walked as much as she could manage. Frequently, she would join Naaman in his chariot. And whenever she must sit or lie down in the wagon, she would invite Atarah and whichever other maidservants were nearby up with her, to give their feet a rest.

Atarah never mentioned how much easier this trip was than the march she had been forced on in the opposite direction over two years ago. Their pace was slower, her ankle was not injured, there were no ropes binding any of them together, and when they made camp each night, there was a nearly festive atmosphere.

And now, after weeks of travel, here they were. Samaria. Israel. Her homeland, if not her home itself.

They had paused a mile outside the city to arrange the caravan per Naaman's direction. He would lead the way inside the walled city on the donkey he had brought for this express purpose—horses were for generals who were about war. Donkeys were a symbol of peace. And he had expressed gladness that the women and children in their party would further that impression. No one brought his wife and tiny heirs along on a raid or invasion. They would offset the show of force his guards and soldiers would represent, casting them instead as something to be respected, not simply feared.

Another minute and they were passing through the open gates. Atarah craned her neck around, trying to commit every bit she could see to memory. From her left, she spotted a group of women around a well. Some chattering, others singing as they raised their filled pots to their heads and started for home.

"LORD, who may abide in Your tabernacle?
Who may dwell in Your holy hill?
He who walks uprightly,
And works righteousness,
And speaks the truth in his heart...."

Atarah sang along with them, the familiar melody tripping off her tongue with a new joy. It had been years since she had sung with other women. Ramina often whispered along with her, but that was the most she could do. And the children would join her, but they had more enthusiasm than ability to match her melody.

Tavi, walking a few steps ahead in his place as right-corner guard of the wagon, shot her a warm look. Not a smile—certainly not while he was on duty—but as close as one could get without moving one's lips. He must know how it filled her to get to sing praises to the Lord again with others.

She added her usual flourishes and trills, grinning down at Malak as he swung their joined hands in time to the beat and joined in.

Midway through the next stanza, the other voices fell silent. At first she thought they had simply gone out of earshot—but no. When she glanced over her shoulder, they were still there in the square. Staring at them. At her and Malak.

It was not the first time other voices had hushed when she had joined them. In Ramah, it had happened often enough that Imma had to explain to her that it was because they wanted to listen, not because they wanted *her* to stop as well.

But none of the faces in Ramah had ever been sneering like these women were now.

Her song faltered and died, just in time for her to see one of the women spit at them and another shout, "David's psalms are not for foreign swine to sing!"

Outrage flared up. Foreign! She was no more foreign than any of them, and surely they could see that. Then she realized their glares were aimed at Malak—sweet, tiny little Malak who looked up at her with complete innocence. Which only made that flare burn brighter.

"Why did you stop, Atarah?"

He must not have heard the women—or perhaps did not understand their accent. Praise be to the Lord for that kindness. She huffed out a breath and pulled him forward another step, even with Tavi, and moved him to her other hand so he was protected between them. She could not imagine anyone actually lashing out at him physically...but then, she had no idea how hard on Samaria the Syrian raids had been these last two years. Perhaps seeing their enemies parading through their streets would push some of them too far, even when it was clearly a delegation of peace.

"Atarah?"

She mustered a smile for the boy. "Sorry, little sweet. I was distracted. So many new sights to see, yes?"

He could probably see very little now, surrounded as he was by taller people, but he simply nodded his agreement and faced forward again.

Atarah met Tavi's gaze though. The smile had vanished from his eyes as surely as it had fled her lips. She did not care to think of what those women were muttering under their breaths now, but she had a feeling they were not looking at her as a daughter of the land finally returned home.

They looked at her as a traitor. Not just for belonging to a Syrian house but for speaking of their king, their history, their God in that house. Defiling what was holy.

A chill shivered through her. She had not, had she? She had taught them with reverence for the Most High. She had sought to honor Him. And was it not to His glory when the Gentiles recognized His word as truth?

"Atarah—stop. You have done no wrong here."

Tavi's quiet words were a balm, but they could not totally erase the injury of those sneers. Not when she spotted dozens of similar expressions as they walked toward the king's house.

They paused before the doors of the mighty abode as Naaman announced himself and stated that he had a letter of introduction for Joram from Ben-Hadad the Second, king of Aram-Damascus. And then they waited. And waited some more. And waited long enough that Malak climbed up with his mother and sister, and even Atarah had grown bored of staring at everything within sight.

At long last, the doors opened again and the same servant who had taken the message inside forever ago emerged with a bow to invite Naaman and his family inside.

Naaman turned to them. They had already gone over what he expected to happen and who would go into the king's house with him—Ramina and the children, Atarah as her attendant, Tavi and Seena and two others to guard the family. Naaman would walk at the head, no guards with him, as a show of peace. At his nod, they helped Ramina and the little ones from the wagon and followed him through the doors, into the cool interior.

The cedar and gold trim she saw were about what she had expected—and, surprisingly, no grander than Naaman's house. She had expected, if ever she stepped foot in the home of a king, to feel awed by it. Small. Instead, it felt surprisingly familiar, a mixture of the familiarity of Israel with the familiarity of a wealthy home.

When they entered the king's receiving chamber, however, that sense of peace fled. The king stood before them, the way his robes swirled about his ankles making her think he had just turned their way quickly. And he looked anything but happy to see them. She could think of no single word that would capture the expression on his face. Not exactly anger or wrath, not exactly fear or outrage. But something far closer to one of those than to the welcome they had hoped for.

Naaman immediately went down on one knee, his head bowed in respect. "King Joram. I thank you for granting me an audience. If it would please your majesty, I have a letter of introduction from my king, Ben-Hadad." He held up the scroll, sealed with wax and pressed with Ben-Hadad's signet.

A servant stepped forward to take the scroll from Naaman and deliver it to Joram's outstretched hand.

As he read it, his face relaxed into somewhat normal lines, at least momentarily. Enough that Atarah could study him surreptitiously and try to take his measure. And to wonder at how strange it was that she had never thought to even see the face of her own king, yet she had been in the same room as Ben-Hadad several times over the last two years.

Joram was far younger than the Syrian king, she knew. His hair had no gray in it, nor did his beard, and there was a youth to his form she had not expected.

Then he finished reading, looked up, and that glimpse of Joram-the-man vanished again behind what was clearly a king who felt heavily put upon. "Are you quite serious?"

An older man eased forward. "My king?"

Joram spun to face who was probably an advisor. "Ben-Hadad writes to me of this general of his who has leprosy, whom he is sending to me for healing! For *healing*!" He seized his outer garment with both hands and ripped. "You are witness! You see how the king of Syria seeks a fight with me! As if I am God, that I can heal!"

Atarah darted a glance at Tavi, who looked just as surprised by the king's reaction as she felt. What exactly had Ben-Hadad written in that letter? No one had ever intimated that the *king* should be the one to heal him. Was that truly what he had implied?

Naaman looked up, though he did not rise—Joram had never given him permission to. "My lord, if I may—"

"You may not." The king was pacing, the beautifully woven cloth now dangling strangely over his tunic. His hands were in his hair. "This is untenable. I must consider what I am to do." He spun to face them again, face livid. "After all I have done to seek peace with that man! Is it not enough that he sends his raiders across our borders continually, stealing the fat of the land? Now he seeks an outright war?"

Naaman bowed his head again, but the hand resting on his knee had fisted. "Though I dare not to speak for my king, my lord, I can speak for myself and assure you that I have come only with peace in my heart."

Joram snorted and waved that away. "I must consider what options I have. Abram, show the general and his family to guest quarters. Those in here with him now may remain under my roof—the rest of your group, General, will kindly wait outside the city for my decision."

"Of course."

The king spun to his advisor again. "Call the rest of the council. Now."

In a flurry of movements, they were ushered—forced, really—back into the corridor by an ashen-faced servant who led them quickly away from the king's chambers and toward a part of the house far removed from where they had been.

The door closed behind them with a bang, not so much as a promise of food and water coming from the servant before he vanished.

Atarah urged Ramina to take a seat. Her mistress stared at Naaman. The children huddled against her sides. Atarah looked from Seena to Tavi and then to the master, who still faced the door as if expecting it to open again.

It was Malak who voiced what they were probably all thinking. "Who will send for Elisha?"

Naaman sighed. "From the looks of it, my son, no one. Elisha will never even be told we are here."

Tavi jerked awake, pulse pounding and breath coming fast. It took him a long moment to remember where he was and why he slept on a stone floor instead of the pallet on the ground that he had called his own for the past weeks of travel. It took another moment still to identify what it was that had awakened him when the first breath of dawn barely brightened the window.

Footsteps? Hurried ones.

He sat up, his gaze drawn to movement across the room. Naaman must have been disturbed by the same sound. He had eased to his feet, silent as a mountain lion.

Footsteps were probably nothing to concern them—a servant about his business or one of the king's many children out for a bit of mischief. Yet even as he tried to dismiss it, Tavi was pushing himself up and pulling his sandals on. Something stirred inside his chest. Perhaps it was only the residue of a dream or the urgency that always came with a sudden awakening, but he did not think so. It felt...different. It felt like it did when the Lord put words into his mouth, thoughts into his head.

*Follow them.*

He put a finger to his lips but then motioned for Naaman to join him. When he tugged at the ring on the door, he was surprised to feel it give under his hand. He knew for a fact they had been locked in last night—it had caused them no little bit of outrage. They had been fed a veritable feast and given extra bedding. Then they had been escorted outside to see to their personal needs. But then the door had been locked.

It was not locked now. Perhaps whoever had rushed by had granted them freedom. Whatever the case, he and Naaman slipped into the hallway and eased the door closed behind them again, then padded silently down the corridor in the direction the footsteps had gone.

He caught a glimpse of a young man turning the corner that would lead to the same chamber they had first been received in yesterday. Tavi frowned, not at the direction but at the man. He looked familiar. Not someone he knew particularly well, but...had he not been at one of the schools? Tavi could not recall his name, but they had passed an evening together when Elisha had first taken Tavi under his wing, being of an age as they were. They had sat there for hours on the banks of the Jordan, tossing pebbles into the waters and speaking of what life was like as a Son of the Prophets.

What was one of the Sons doing here? At this hour?

There was one way to find out. Tavi picked up his pace, knowing Naaman would match it.

The visitor did not knock upon the king's door. He simply pushed it open and left it so, dropping to a knee once inside.

Tavi and Naaman pressed themselves to the shadows cloaking the walls. Joram was within, looking so haggard that it was clear he had not slept at all. A few advisors clustered around him, no better off. They all stared at the young man who had burst in upon them.

The king stood. "Who are you? And how did you get in here? I thought I said the door was to be locked!" He cast a glare toward the corner of the room, presumably at a servant. Tavi could only imagine how pale the poor recipient of the look must have gone.

"It—it *was*, my king! I swear it!" came the squeak of a reply.

Interesting. So had their own been. Perhaps this fellow had *not* unlocked it. Perhaps the King of kings had.

The young prophet kept to his knee. "The prophet said to tell you, 'What is a locked door to the God Who Sees?'"

"The prophet." Joram tossed down the scroll he had been clutching. "Elisha? Elisha sent you?"

"The Prophet heard from the Lord last night, O king, and has sent me to say, 'Why have you torn your clothes? Please let the man with leprosy come to me, and he shall know that there is a prophet in Israel.'"

A shout went up from inside the chamber. Tavi could not discern words so much as tone—the king, jubilant and relieved. Several of the advisors, incredulous. One other, joyous.

Tavi looked back at his master, who wore a stunned half smile on his lips. Tavi offered a full one of his own. "And there is the answer to your son's question, my father—no man needs to tell Elisha that we are here. God Himself informs the prophet of everything he needs to know."

# CHAPTER ELEVEN

Atarah kept pace beside the chariot, though she darted a glance over her shoulder frequently to make sure Malak and Lilya still slept peacefully in the bed of the wagon. They had worn themselves out with celebration that morning as they left Samaria, leaving them both exhausted after a poor night's sleep. Just as well—the time would pass quickly for them now, and when they awoke, their party would be at Elisha's house.

*Elisha's house.* The words still brought a thrill to her heart, though she had already recited them dozens, perhaps hundreds of times since Tavi and Naaman had burst into their quarters that morning with the news.

The prophet knew they were here, though no man had told him. The prophet had sent for them.

The excitement of it left no room in her mind for disappointment over the fact that Elisha was not near Ramah—he was here, at his home outside Samaria. He was *here*, and they would see him today. Or Naaman would, anyway. Who was to say whether she herself would lay eyes on him? But that hardly mattered. Her master would surely be healed, for why else would Elisha have called for him?

Ramina rode in the chariot that her husband was driving, her arm wrapped through his and her face absolutely rapturous. "I knew it," she said for the twentieth time since they had finally gotten their entourage moving and began following the young man who had come to guide them to the prophet. "I knew the prophet would see you. He will make you whole again, my love."

Never had Atarah seen Naaman smile as much as he had been doing that morning. "How do you suppose he will do it? A word? A touch?"

Atarah's lips twitched into a quick grin of their own. She looked up at where Tavi marched beside her—he too had been smiling when he and Naaman had reentered their room that morning, long enough and bright enough that Ramina had taken note of it and whispered to Atarah with a teasing grin that she had never realized how handsome he was.

He was not smiling now though. Nor was he watching the horizon for the first glimpse of Elisha's home. His eyes, though mostly trained straight ahead, kept darting to the other side of the master's chariot.

To another not-smiling form. Ram, who had been glowering ever since they set off. Though she had with her own ears heard the master direct other guards to take up position around his chariot, Ram had somehow taken the place of one of them, and the general had not even seemed to notice, so distracted was he with his task.

But Ram would have heard every exchange between Naaman and Ramina. Every hope, every prayer.

Her own euphoria settled into something more cautious.

Ramina seemed as oblivious to her cousin's presence as her husband was. "In the stories Atarah has told us, the Lord and His prophets have worked in many different ways. When Moses parted the Red Sea, it was by stretching out his staff toward the waters."

"I recall that one, from the songs the children sing." Naaman nodded, his gaze distant but bright. "He will call on the name of the Lord his God, of course. Perhaps stretch his hand over the spot of leprosy."

"I imagine we will be able to watch it vanish before our very eyes." Ramina bounced much like her children were wont to do, hugging Naaman's good arm. "Did I not tell you, my husband? The God of Israel is the God Who Heals, as Atarah said. His prophet will make you whole as the priests of Rimmon could never do."

Atarah did not need Tavi's example this time—she glanced over at Ram on her own in time to see the clouds of disapproval gather on his face. No, *disapproval* was too kind a word. Hatred, that was the only one strong enough. Whether on behalf of his god or because he knew that a restoration of Naaman's health would spell disaster to his own ambitions, his hatred for the couple in the chariot increased more obviously with each word they spoke.

Ramina laughed in her quiet, breathy way. "Of course, when Moses drew water from the rock, he struck it." She bumped her hip into Naaman's. "Perhaps the prophet will strike you and make the leprosy run away in fear."

Naaman laughed along with her. "Perhaps so. Though I imagine something more befitting a man of his ilk. Stretching his hand out, perhaps waving it over the spot seems far more likely. I wonder what his face will look like when he does it. Will we be able to see the glory of his God on his countenance?"

Ramina grew calmer, her own face more contemplative. "I hope so. I have seen the fury of Rimmon—I long to see power now of a different sort. From all Atarah has said, her God is not like ours. He acts from perfect justice but also perfect love. I can only imagine what that looks like."

Atarah glanced at Tavi again. They *did* know what it looked like, if they paused to realize it. They had seen it in Tavi's eyes as surely as she had when he told Naaman the message on his heart.

Ramina turned to her. "Your father is a lesser prophet, is he not? And you have met Elisha. What does he look like when your God speaks to him?"

Atarah could not help but flick another cautious glance at Ram. He kept his face forward, but even so she could see the ticking in his jaw. He was listening, filing away every word.

Still, she would answer her mistress. "He looks, for the most part, like any other man, my lady. He is kind and thoughtful. But when the Spirit is whispering to him—which happens far more often than to prophets like my father, I grant you—you can see it in his eyes. I always liken it to fire. To light. The kind that gives life and heat, but which can blaze, blind, and destroy too. Power, reined in but ready to be set loose if the Lord commands it."

For the first time, Ram actually turned toward them. "Well, surely for a general as renowned as Naaman, this God of yours will put on a show. He is in effect demonstrating His power for Syria itself, is He not?" His lips curled into a smirk. "Whatever happens today, we will return to Damascus with stories of it. If anything could inspire a deity to show Himself great, it ought to be that."

Naaman did not look all that startled at realizing his rival was there at his side. He pursed his lips. "You may have a point, Ram. Surely this Yahweh will want to prove Himself more powerful than Rimmon in some indisputable, visible way. As He showed the Egyptians and their gods."

Ramina let loose a laugh. "How blessed are we, that we will get to behold it!"

Something like unease stirred in Atarah's chest. She looked at Tavi again to see if he felt it too—though of course, he was always harder to read than she was. She thought she saw a shift in his eyes though. Enough of one that she said, "If I may speak, my lady?"

The mistress beamed down at her. "Of course you may!"

She drew in a long breath. "Elijah was the predecessor of Elisha, his mentor. It was he who served the Lord during the reign of the wicked King Ahab and his wife Jezebel. One day, there was a great showdown between him and the priests of Ba'al."

Ramina's eyes sparkled. "And your Yahweh won."

"He did. With a spectacular show of fire from heaven, so great that it devoured the offering, the altar, and many gallons of water that Elijah had instructed them to pour out upon it before he called on the Lord. After the priests of Ba'al had first spent the entire day trying to get their god to send down fire, to no avail."

Ramina grinned. "More proof of His power."

"Yes. But afterward, Jezebel sought Elijah to kill him, and he fled. The Lord sustained him in the wilderness, and then he instructed Elijah to stand on the mountain before the Lord. A great and strong wind tore into the mountain and broke the rocks to pieces—but according to the report Elijah told of it, God was not in the wind. So then the earth shook—but God was not in the earthquake. And after the earthquake, a fire came and swirled all around him—but the Lord was not in the fire."

Ramina's face calmed by degrees as Atarah spoke, soft understanding lighting her eyes. "So where *was* the Lord?"

"In a still, small voice that spoke in the wake of these things. God was in the whisper."

Naaman frowned at her. "I do not understand."

Atarah sighed. "Sometimes, my father, God shows Himself in the most stunning of displays—and sometimes He works in the quiet of our own hearts. Perhaps Elisha will have you perform some great feat. Or—"

"We are here." The student who had been leading them appeared before the chariot. He gave a short bow and motioned to the house situated just a little ways off in a grove of graceful trees. It was larger than most they had passed in the neighborhood, no doubt because he had quite a few students studying at his feet, like the young man who had led them here. She could glimpse them moving about the olive trees, and a few were at work on one of the outbuildings. She did not spot a figure who looked like Elisha from here—he could be anywhere within the compound, or even somewhere in the countryside. Elisha had been known before to call someone into his presence and then make them wait hours or even days while he sought the Lord. Patience, he always said, was one of the Almighty's favorite virtues.

Naaman pulled his horses to a halt and secured the reins, Atarah clearly forgotten. He leaped to the ground. "Tavi, Ram, with me. My love, stay back a bit with Atarah. If the Lord sends fire from heaven, I would have you and the children safe from it."

Atarah sighed. If the Lord sent fire from heaven, it could consume any of them He willed, proximity notwithstanding.

Naaman strode toward the towering doorway to the compound, Tavi and Ram both following him a step behind. Atarah held out a hand to help Ramina from the chariot, which swayed a bit as the horses shifted.

Her mistress held her hand tight. "I intend to hear everything that is said. We will stay back but within earshot."

"You will get no arguments from me." They both looked back to make sure that Dafna was still watching over the children, and she gave them a smile and a wave to let them know all was well. Careful to stay out of Naaman's view, they scurried forward, to the protection of cypress trees nearby.

A man was coming toward Naaman, but it was not Elisha, nor was it Gehazi. Whatever his name, he stopped a stone's throw from Naaman and greeted him with a bow. "Good afternoon, General."

Naaman bowed in return. "Good afternoon. I have come, at his request, to present myself to the prophet Elisha."

The man nodded. "The prophet sends this message to you—go and wash in the Jordan seven times, and your flesh shall be restored to you, and you shall be clean."

Silence pulsed, broken only by the tweeting of a bird somewhere in the olive grove. Atarah drew a breath slowly into her lungs, afraid to so much as move.

Ram was the first to break the stillness by crossing his arms over his chest. "Is the old seer not aware of who this is? Naaman, the most powerful general in the Syrian army, who has more wealth just in his wagon than all of Israel combined! And does this so-called prophet not even show him the respect of coming out to greet him himself?"

Atarah's every muscle tensed. She had not actually thought any fire would be raining from heaven—but to insult the prophet of the Most High in his own home could be a dangerous business.

And Naaman did not turn to rebuke the impertinence.

Elisha's messenger did not even blink out of turn. "The prophet sent that message and that message only—bathe seven times in the Jordan."

Naaman spun away, toward them though he did not seem to see them, his chest heaving. "The River Jordan? *This* is what the God of Israel instructs? I had thought the prophet would come out to me himself! That he would wave his hand over my arm and call on the name of the Lord."

Tavi stepped toward him. "My father—"

"The Jordan! Are not the Abanah and the Pharpar, the rivers of Damascus, better than all the waters of Israel? Could I not wash in them and be clean, if simply bathing was all that was required to be healed of this leprosy?" Face mottled, Naaman strode away from the door, back toward the chariot.

Tavi jogged to keep up with him, Ram hurrying along as well. Their two faces were exact opposites—one a dark satisfaction and the other a light-filled plea.

Atarah and Ramina dashed back to the chariot to meet them. Naaman looked ready to leap in and storm all the way back to Damascus, powered only by his own frustration.

"This was a waste of time," Ram spat out as they all converged on the chariot. "Did I not warn you that chasing after another god would be useless—and worse, anger Rimmon? This God of Israel is so worthless that even His priests do not dare to look you in the face."

"Prophet," Tavi corrected, "not priest. And please, my father"—Tavi stepped in front of Naaman before he could climb into the chariot, his hands up and palms out, begging him to hold—"you had your ideas, I know, of what you thought would happen. But did you not hear the story Atarah was telling you about Elijah? Sometimes God is not in the whirlwind or the earthquake or the firestorm. Sometimes He is in the whisper. Sometimes He works through quiet, simple means."

Naaman just grunted.

Ram sneered. "He fails to work at all, you mean. Wash in a river? What sort of idiot thinks that could possibly heal leprosy?"

Tavi did not so much as glance at Ram. He kept his gaze on Naaman. "My father, if the prophet had told you to do something great, would you not have done it?"

Naaman's shoulders eased down a notch. "Of course I would have. I would have scaled a mountain, gone on a year-long quest, brought him any sacrifice he requested."

Tavi spread his hands wide. "How much more then, when he says to you to wash and be clean? It is a simple thing. A quiet thing. It is a thing that does not require your strength or your prowess—but only your faith. Faith that *He* will work through this unassuming water, not that you will earn this healing by your own bravery. This is about Yahweh Rapha, my lord, and your willingness to believe He is truly the Most High. That is all."

Naaman sighed and let his gaze fall to the ground.

Atarah eased a step forward too. "Please, my lord. As Tavi says—it is a simple thing that is asked of you. If you would do the great task, why would you shun the easy one?"

His lips pursed.

Ramina glided to his side and slipped her hand into his. "I believe, my love. I believe He is the Most High. I believe you need only to obey to be healed."

With a sigh, Naaman gazed into his wife's eyes. Would capitulation be enough, if it led to obedience? Or did he too have to truly believe in order to receive his healing?

Ram let out a sound of disgust. "This is absurd. A disgrace to your family and an affront to Syria and Rimmon. We should leave immediately and—"

"No." Naaman spoke quietly, but there was no arguing with the authority in his tone. He lifted Ramina's hand and kissed it, then stepped away, shoulders squared. "How far to the River Jordan?"

"Not far," Tavi answered.

Ram sputtered. "You cannot be serious!"

"Enough, Ram." Naaman stepped into the chariot when Tavi moved out of the way, urging Ramina to stay on solid ground. "If it does not work, then I am out only the hour or two it will take me to get to the river and bathe. Such a small inconvenience is worth the affront to my pride. But if it does work—then we will know, will we not? We will know if the God of Israel is who He says He is."

Ramina grinned over at Atarah. "He is. That is even the name He gave to Moses, is it not? I Am."

Naaman motioned Seena forward. "Stay here with my family and the rest of the household and ask permission to set up camp for the night. There is no need to take everyone to the river. Tavi knows the way, it seems."

Tavi nodded. "I stayed a week here with the prophet before he took me to Ramah. I can take you to the river, my father."

"Can I not come with you?" Ramina reached for her husband's hand again, though she did not make an attempt to join him in the chariot.

He smiled gently down at her. "The children will be stirring any moment. And I suspect Atarah would like the chance to seek someone among the prophet's house who has news of her family. But I will not be long, I promise you. And if I am healed, you will see the miracle with your own eyes soon enough."

But if he was not, he did not want her to witness the first disappointment—that was what Atarah read in his eyes.

Ramina likely saw the same. She relented with a nod and stepped away, offering him a smile. "Go with God, my husband. We will be praying for you here."

With a derisive snort, Ram stalked off, toward the soldiers milling about behind them.

Good. With any luck, they would not see him again for the rest of the day.

Tavi stood beside Naaman on the banks of the Jordan—the waters that meant home. Perhaps it was not the grandest river in the world, but that hardly mattered. It was the river that flowed through the Promised Land. The river Joshua had parted as Moses had the Red Sea. The river that fed them all.

Naaman drew in a sharp breath. "So how does this work, do you think? Will it improve a bit with each dip? Do I have to submerge only my arm, or my whole body?"

Tavi's lips twitched. "Generally when one says 'bathe,' one is speaking of one's whole self."

"I agree." In proof, Naaman bent down and began untying his sandals. "I will wade into the river, dunk myself entirely, rub down as I would any other time, and reemerge. We will call that once."

It made fine sense to Tavi. "As for whether it will heal you incrementally or all at once at the end, I cannot say, my lord. The Lord will work as He will work. We cannot know how—but we can trust that He will."

With a nervous-looking nod, Naaman removed his cloak, his gloves, all his outer clothing, leaving only the short tunic he wore underneath. "Count with me? I do not want to do something foolish like lose count and so lose my healing."

"You have my word, my father."

With another sharply indrawn breath, Naaman waded into the river. It would be cold this time of year, but he did not flinch. He strode steadily into it until the waters came just above his waist, and then he crouched down and disappeared under the waters. He came up scrubbing. And shivering, Tavi saw when he stepped out onto the banks again.

"One."

Again Naaman went in, dunked, and scrubbed.

"Two."

On "three," Tavi noted that the patch of leprosy on his arm had not changed, but the rest of him had, likely just from the cold water. Naaman was pale, his lips turning purple from the cold.

Back he went again.

"Lord God Almighty," Tavi prayed quietly as Naaman dipped again, "I know You will do as You promised, according to the word of Elisha. Give us the hearts to believe."

Naaman came out shivering. "Four?"

"Four."

He vanished again, and Tavi closed his eyes. "You are the God Who Heals. You are the God Who Sees. You are I Am." He opened his eyes again just as Naaman sloshed out. "Five."

Naaman looked down at his arm. The skin looked puckered, red at the edges, waterlogged. But clearly not restored. His shoulders sagged a bit, but he splashed back into the river.

"Six," Tavi said when he stepped out again. "Once more, my lord."

Naaman paused though, clearly trying to catch the breath the cold water had stolen from him. He looked again at his arm. "I thought..."

That it would look better each time? That there would be something measurable to give him hope? Tavi moved to his side and clasped a hand to his frigid, dripping elbow. "Who are we to know the mind of the Lord? To question His ways? Once more, my father. Go in and be healed."

Naaman's eyes met his, and Tavi saw in them all the things he had kept hidden so long—his pain, his insecurity, his doubt. His fear that this disease would eat him whole, destroy all he had fought for, ruin the family he loved more than life. "What if it fails to work?" His whisper was more broken than any of Ramina's.

Tavi held his elbow firmly. "It will not fail. The prophet has spoken, and he does not speak amiss. Faith over fear, Father."

Naaman held his gaze for a long moment and then clasped Tavi's arm in return. "Faith over fear, my son."

He turned back to the Jordan.

# CHAPTER TWELVE

The music of the prophet's house was as sweet as the fragrance wafting on the breeze from the cook fires. In the distance, someone strummed a lyre in an old familiar melody. No voice paired with it in song that she could hear, but the wind sang its praises to the Lord. Happy voices shouted to one another in the olive grove. Laughter punctuated the gurgle of a stream that must feed into the river.

Atarah had helped Ramina and Dafna feed the children, who had indeed woken up minutes after Naaman and Tavi left. She had sung them a few songs, to soothe Ramina as much as to entertain the little ones. But then her mistress had bid her go and see if she could find someone with the answers she sought.

Her heart skipped as she walked away from their encampment and toward Elisha's house. She had no idea if they would let her inside, if she would find anyone she knew, if anyone even had the answers she prayed for. But she had been given the gift of seeking them, and so she would take it.

But where to start? She paused at the edge of the courtyard, just taking a moment to absorb all the familiar activity. Children—all boys, no doubt students—scurried around doing chores, a few maidservants joked and laughed as they stirred an enormous pot and checked the bread that she could smell baking, and men of various ages moved frequently into and out of the house, no doubt all about the work of Elisha.

She could imagine so easily that this was the school she had called home most of her life. That her father was somewhere inside, that her mother was one of the immas laughing over the cook fire, that her own siblings were chasing the others about. She could close her eyes and be instantly home, where the Word of the Lord was served along with her daily bread, feeding her soul as well as her belly.

A song whispered to life, using the music from the lyre as a backdrop more than instruction on what her own melody should be. Words soon matched it note for note—not words that she had learned at Imma's knee, penned already by David or the Sons of Korah or any of the other psalmists.

Her own words, penned by her own heart. *Beside the waters You lead me, O Lord, by the waters that make me whole.*

She sang a few of them, waiting to see what other lyrics would join the melody. Before any more could surface, though, movement in her periphery grabbed her attention. Familiar movement. She turned her head, her lips parting with grateful shock when she realized that the older man approaching the house from the olive grove was none other than Gehazi—her father's oldest, dearest friend. The man more likely than any but Elisha himself to know what had happened that day in Ramah. He had been there, she had seen him! He would know what had become of her family.

"Gehazi!" His name spilled from her lips in a shout even as her feet kicked up into a run.

He paused outside the circle of the courtyard, looking around to see who had called him. His vision had always been weak, and it was not until she was nearly upon him, laughing, that his eyes widened in recognition. "Atarah?"

Recognition...but where was the joy? Eclipsed by the surprise, no doubt. She nearly threw herself into his arms as she had always done as a child, but he stumbled back a step, so she halted a few feet away from him. "Gehazi, praise the Lord! I was hoping I would see you. From the moment we stepped foot into Israelite territory, it has been my prayer."

"We?" His gaze flicked from her to the camp behind her and darkened like the rainy season's skies. "How exactly do you come to be here, Atarah? With whom? We thought you dead."

They had? She sucked in a sharp breath. Part of her wanted to take hope from that "we"—did it include her family? But another part wanted to weep at the thought of her parents mourning her, when all along she was being led captive to Damascus.

She motioned behind her, at the collection of Syrians going about their own meal preparation. "I was taken prisoner. I have been serving these two years, along with Tavi, in the house of Naaman, a general in the Syrian army. I am his wife's companion."

"A Syrian general." He stared at her blankly for a moment, and then he hissed out a breath. "*The* Syrian general? The one who is here for healing?"

"Yes!" Laughter bubbled up again and spilled out. "Is it not the strangest thing? All the stories I have told his wife and children of Yahweh these two years convinced them to seek Elisha for a healing."

Fire snapped in his eyes—not the kind she was used to seeing in a prophet's, but angry, burning. Before she could even register what he was doing, his hand snaked out and slapped her viciously across the cheek. "Foolish girl! What have you done?"

A cry of pain escaped at the impact, and her hand flew to cover her stinging flesh. She staggered back, out of reach. Nearly two and a half years she had been a slave, but this was the first time in her life anyone had ever struck her in the face. She stared aghast at the man she had always considered an uncle. "What? What have I done?"

"What have you *done*?" Though his voice was little more than a low hiss, it sounded like thunder reverberating through her soul. "Can you be so stupid? They are our enemies! The enemies of our God! And you—you have brought them here, not to seek their destruction, but to seek *healing* for their leader? As if the God of gods will not strike the man dead for his audacity—He will probably strike *you* as well, and you would deserve it."

"But I…" Her words died away in a swirl of confusion. She had done nothing wrong, had she? She had only sung His praises. Was that not what they were supposed to do? To extol the Lord in a foreign land?

Gehazi paced a step away. "I could not fathom, when I heard he was here, how he had even learned that there was a prophet in Israel capable of such miracles. But this—that you, the daughter of my oldest friend, were the one to betray us—it is unthinkable! Unacceptable!"

Betrayed them? The world tilted, and she groped for something to steady her. Finding nothing, she sank to the ground. "I have betrayed no one."

Gehazi spun back to face her, pointing a wild finger in the direction of the Syrians. "He is the very general who led the raid against the school in Ramah! Do you not realize that?"

Her cheek burned with his accusation. She could scarcely find her voice to answer him. "Of course I do."

"What excuse do you have then?" He crouched down, his face close enough to hers that she could see the spittle gathering in the corners of his mouth, the red veins in his eyes. "Why have you not been praying that the Lord would curse him and his entire army for what they have done to the people of God?"

"I..." What could she say? Had God not promised that He would send them these very hardships if they fell away from His Law, abandoned His covenant? And had not Israel and Judah both been rife with idolatries for generations? Her family, those of the schools were some of the few who had remained faithful through the reigns of king after evil king, all of whom led the people astray.

God had delivered so many of them into the hands of their enemies as a curse on *them*, and as a warning.

But that did not mean He favored the enemies. Of course not. Israel might have gone astray, but at least a remnant of them knew who the true God was. The same could not be said for those of Aram-Damascus. But even so. "Did Joseph not serve Pharaoh with loyalty and speak to him of the Most High?"

"And now you would compare yourself to the patriarchs themselves?" Gehazi shoved back to his feet. "You are a disgrace to your father's name—it would be better if you really were dead, as they have long believed you to be. If anyone knew that you have been defiling yourself in the house of a pagan, it would break your mother's heart. Ruin your sisters' chances for a good marriage. Mar your brother's hopes of rising to a high position in the king's court, now that he is a scribe. And your father." He shook his head and spat at her. "He would curse the day you were born if ever he heard of this."

He stormed off, and Atarah watched him go through eyes blurry with tears. Her whole body shook, as if it had been his foot that connected with her arm instead of his saliva. She wrapped her arms around her knees and rocked back and forth, willing her breath to come evenly instead of in these ragged gasps. Willing the tears to leave. Willing the hateful words to stop bombarding her mind anew every second.

What had she done? She had only tried to serve Him, to honor Him, to remember Him. She only tried, as Tavi had exhorted her, to be who He created her to be.

But Gehazi was second only to Elisha—he had been serving him since Elijah was caught up into heaven. He might very well be the next great prophet after Elisha eventually rested in the bosom of Abraham. He had more wisdom than she could ever hope, a better understanding of the ways of the Lord.

If he said she had made herself an enemy of the Almighty, then how could she doubt he spoke the truth?

The tears racked her, shaking her down to her very core. How could she have betrayed what she held most dear without even realizing it? Why had Tavi not known, not warned her—but he had done the same. Did that mean he shared her shame and guilt? Had it not been God's Spirit whispering into his ears at all? Had it been some demon?

She sat there, slumped over on the cold ground, until the sobs gave way to shudders and the shudders to an echoing numbness. By that time twilight crept over the hills, painting the sky with shades of rose and gold and purple—royal hues sent to mock her. She lurched to her feet and stumbled her way back to the camp, not knowing what else to do. What did God expect of her? Want of her? To return to her mistress… or perhaps to wander out into the wilderness and await His judgment? Wild beasts or a fork of lightning would be a fitting end for a traitor.

She was a coward though, clearly. She made for the familiarity of camp and children's laughter, grateful for the cloaking shadows of the coming night that would hide her face from those who would ask too many questions.

No one paid her any mind though—not given that the very moment she reentered the camp, Naaman's chariot came charging in, the horses prancing, their sides lathered and heaving from their run.

Naaman jumped down, tossing Tavi the reins—Tavi, who was grinning like a normal man.

"Ramina!" Naaman cried as held his arm aloft. He laughed even as he shouted. "My wife, come and see what the Lord has done!"

The last rays of the sun caught on his arm.

Gone were the white patches of leprosy. Gone were the cracks and scars from countless battles. Gone, even, were the spots and freckles from so many hours in the relentless sun. His skin looked completely new, soft as a babe's. Not just there on his arm either. Ramina came charging toward him, and he swept her up, spun her in a circle, and gave Atarah a glimpse of his face.

Free of wrinkles. Free of scars. Free of blemishes. Every single flaw in his skin had been restored to perfect health.

She pressed her back against one of the trees on the edge of the camp. What did this mean? Gehazi had sounded so certain that the Lord would strike Naaman down dead for his brazenness in approaching Him. That He would curse him— yet here he stood, healed. Renewed. Restored.

Ramina laughed with unbridled joy, clinging to Naaman's neck. "Praise the Lord!" she shouted. *Shouted.* "His goodness is beyond compare. His mercies endure forever. He is One, and He is God."

"The only God in all the earth." Naaman pulled back, staring at her. "Ramina—your voice."

The mistress's hand flew to her throat, her eyes going wide. "The scar—I do not feel it."

Naaman snatched her hand away. "I do not *see* it." He laughed, as she had a moment ago, and crushed her to his chest. "That was my prayer as I dipped that last time in the Jordan, my love. That Yahweh Rapha would heal not only my arm but every broken thing in my soul. Every one of your scars. That He would make us new creatures, able to raise our children to know His name."

Malak and Lilya finally caught up with their mother, Dafna trailing a step behind.

Atarah slid around the trunk of a tree, wishing it would absorb her into its bark. Maybe then, if she had its hundreds of years of wisdom, she would know how she ought to react to this revelation. Maybe then, with hundreds of years more stretching out before her, she would be able to digest these strange miracles.

She wanted to leap with joy as they were doing. To shout and sing and teach Ramina to sing. She wanted to embrace her mistress and hug Tavi and take her place in the celebration sure to spring up.

But Gehazi's words held her as securely bound as the ropes that had led her away captive.

She slid another step around the tree and then came to an abrupt halt, her very breath freezing in her lungs.

Elisha. He stood not thirty feet away from her, in the shadows of another tree. His familiar mantle draped his shoulders— rumored to be the exact one Elijah had given him, though surely that would have worn out by now, unless God had touched it as He had the clothing of the Israelites during the wandering. He held it closed against the cool evening wind and watched the scene playing out.

A smile nestled in the corners of his lips. Why? Was he actually glad that Naaman had been healed? Or did he know something she did not about the fate yet to befall him?

"I must present myself to the man of God," Naaman declared even then.

Elisha melted deeper into the shadows.

Seena spoke up from farther back. "Not tonight, my lord. The messenger who gave you the instructions was here not half an hour ago and said that you should come to the door again in the morning. The prophet will be about his dinner and his prayers at this hour."

"The morning then. Tonight, we praise the Lord with a celebration of thanksgiving!"

Her eyes slid shut, and when she opened them again, Elisha had vanished.

That sounded like a fine idea. She picked her way from shadow to shadow until she had reached the edge of the copse of trees, where the stream gurgled by. Laughter and shouts rang out from the camp, but they only made her heart ache all the more. She sank down to the ground between the gnarled roots of a giant tree and leaned back against its trunk.

Her parents lived, as did her siblings—but she could curse them by her very life. She could ruin all their chances at happiness. And all because she had chosen this household above her own. Sought their happiness when apparently she ought to have been striving to undermine them. She should have been a spy in Damascus, not a silly girl too eager to sing whatever happy songs she pleased.

Music filled her but not like ever before. This was no bright river—it was a slow, dark swamp. She parted her lips and let the mournful melody slip out.

One of the songs her mother sang. One of the songs that could break a heart of stone.

It broke hers, though she was made of much softer stuff. Too much softer. Her eyes burned, though no more tears filled them. Her throat burned too, with every long, sad note.

Someone settled at her side as she sang the last words, a strong arm pulling her against a strong chest. Her breath caught on a sob. Tavi.

"My sweet songbird—why do you mourn? You, who have always been the very sunshine? Those are not the songs you are meant to sing."

She buried her face in his shoulder, wishing she had saved some of her tears earlier. Perhaps some of this tension in her chest would leave if only she could cry it out. "I saw Gehazi. He said—he said I am a traitor. That it would be better for my family if I had never been born."

"Nonsense." His arms tightened around her, one of his hands stroking her hair. "Do not believe him, Atarah. You were born for a purpose, and I believe you have fulfilled part of it this day. You have had a hand in leading a good man and a good woman to the saving knowledge of the one true God."

Even an hour ago, such words would have lit unspeakable joy in her heart. But what if Gehazi was right? What if her songs had done the unthinkable and dishonored the Lord? "I should never have opened my mouth in song. I should have clung to my silence, as I had sworn to myself I would."

"But then you would not be my Atarah."

"Then I would not be a traitor to Yahweh! They are our enemies, Tavi, and we have helped them. Served them. Loved them—it is surely an abomination in the sight of God, as Gehazi said."

"Atarah, listen to me." He nudged her away just a bit and tilted her chin up with a finger under it. Through the fading embers of day, she could just make out the aqua of his eyes. "What makes an enemy? Is it where he was born or the choices he makes, the direction of his heart? Should Rahab not have been rightfully considered an enemy? Yet she is in the lineage of David."

"But he has attacked our people."

"He has obeyed the orders of his king, yes, and he has in that way been the very hand of God, reminding our people of the price they pay for the idols and Asherah poles they refuse to cut down. But always he sought to preserve lives wherever he could. Always he respected what was sacred. And today he has made a choice that will change the course of his future."

A spark from his eyes settled in her heart. "He is a good man. I have long thought so. And if the Lord has a use for him, then I am glad. But does that excuse me?"

"You need no excusing." He brushed a lock of hair away from her cheek, making her aware of the fact that her headscarf had fallen at some point—it was not even around her shoulders. "You did as you were meant to do. You sang the songs of God's glory, and you sang them with love for Him, as you have always done." His fingers touched her cheek then, no hair as an excuse. "It was the very first thing I came to love about you."

The spark kindled an ember. She could find no words now, nor could she look away from those eyes that held all the depths of the world inside them.

Those eyes that moved over her face as if memorizing it, as if he had not seen her a million times already. "It was what made me know so quickly why Elisha had led me to Ramah and not to one of the other schools."

The ember burst into flame.

Tavi leaned a little closer. "It was what gave me the courage to go to your father—me, an orphan with absolutely nothing to my name—and beg him to let me make you my wife."

The flames might well consume her whole. Her fingers curled into the fabric of his cloak. "You went to my father?"

"I promised him all I had—I could offer no bride-price, but I swore to him my service for as long as he would have me at hand. I swore to him that I would do anything in my power to protect you and give you a life of joy, that I would nurture the song in your heart."

He had loved her? Even then, before all this? Was that why he had jumped in front of Ram that day, why he had traded his own freedom for her? She convinced one hand to let go of his cloak so that she could lift it, trembling, to trace the contours of his jaw. "What did Abba say?"

His lips curved, parted, blooming into the most beautiful smile she had ever seen. "He said he would be honored to call me his son, and that he only wanted the approval of Elisha before he had the covenant drawn up."

The morning of the raid flashed through her mind—the secret in her father's smile, the news he had said he would share with her after the prophet's arrival. He must have been fully convinced that Elisha would approve it. *He* had approved it. This man, the one she had always admired, whose smile she strove to win every day, who had become her dearest friend in the world, had these two years been her betrothed—more or less—and she had not even known it.

"Why did you never tell me?"

"Our world changed so drastically that day. My ability to keep my promise to your father was taken away. I cannot serve him now as I meant to—but I could still protect you. I could still do my all to give you a life of joy."

What then? He meant *not* to marry her because they were Naaman's slaves? But that gleam in his eye was not that of a promise he never meant to fulfill.

He leaned closer still, so close that her heart thundered like a thousand stallions and her breath tangled up with each galloping beat. "What would you have said," he murmured from an inch away, "had your father had the chance to tell you of my proposal?"

*Said?* A breath of laughter huffed from her lips. "I would have sung the most joyful song I could think of—I would have composed one on the spot. There could be no greater honor, Tavi, and no greater joy than being your wife."

His lips caught hers then, holding them captive in a kiss so sweet it made her want to weep for joy, so full of love it made her want to wrap her arms around him and never let him go.

His hands moved to either side of her head, anchoring her there. "I have loved you so long, my Atarah—I will love you until my dying breath."

"Tavi." It was all she managed before he kissed her again. Her head was swimming with the most beautiful delirium by the time he pulled away again. What had she been about to say? Oh yes. "I love you with the light of a billion stars. I love you with every note I could ever sing."

He kissed her once more and then rested his forehead on hers. "Do you trust me, Atarah?"

It might well be the most ridiculous question he had ever asked. "With my life, my heart, and my very soul."

"Then believe me when I say that we will marry—but we will marry in Ramah, with your imma lowering the veil over your face and your abba giving you to me. I will keep my word to him."

She pulled back a little, her racing heart fluttering in her chest. Her parents thought she was dead—would wish it, according to Gehazi. Yet here was this man she loved, promising her a family restored. "You think we will make it back there?"

"I think our God is one who believes in the sanctity of a covenant. And I believe in my heart of hearts that He will enable me to uphold my end. I do not know how, or how long it may take. Will you wait with me? For me?"

He believed. He believed from the start that God would make a way for them. That they could serve Him even in Damascus. He believed that the God Who Sees had put them exactly where He wanted them to be and that He would someday deliver them home.

He believed in what Gehazi could not even fathom—and he believed it so fully that he convinced the most powerful general in the Syrian forces of its truth. He believed so much that now Naaman believed, and Ramina.

She gripped his wrists, holding him as surely as he held her. "I will wait as long as it takes. And in the meantime, we will serve this family who has seen the power of the Lord today, and we will teach them all we can about His wondrous ways."

Perhaps Gehazi would curse her for it.

But Elisha had seen—and Elisha had smiled on them. That was the only note she needed to listen to, and it rang as clear as a clarion. Gehazi's voice was just noise, like cymbals clanging out of turn.

"Come." She tugged on his wrists, the music so loud in her ears she was unsure whether it came from her own mind or in the camp. "We have a celebration to enjoy."

# CHAPTER THIRTEEN

A tarah lifted Lilya onto her hip, smiling at the way the little one rubbed her eyes. Even she had stayed up too late last night, clapping to the music and dancing with her brother until they both collapsed in an exhausted heap. Yet at the first light of dawn, their parents were up and waking the rest of them too.

Actually, Atarah was not altogether convinced Naaman and Ramina had ever slept. She had still heard them whispering together as she drifted off, and that had not been nearly enough hours ago. But one would never guess at their sleeplessness to look at their faces. Radiant, that was what they were. Glowing with the joy of the Lord.

Naaman stood now before the entirety of his people. They were all silent, awaiting his word. He lifted a hand. "I want to thank you all for taking this journey with me. For sharing our joy last night. But this blessing from the Lord of All will come with a cost, and I do not know yet what it will be. I do know this, however—there is no room for any idols in our midst. If you have brought one with you, I will ask you to destroy it now, knowing that I will compensate you for its price."

He paused, and a ripple of disbelief moved through the crowd. Especially among the soldiers, all of whom probably carried a talisman of some sort with them. "I know this sounds odd to you—but this God is a jealous God. I assure you, any remnants of other gods will be removed from my own house the moment we return to it. If you are unwilling to comply with this, then you have my permission to depart now for home."

No one immediately stomped off, but that hardly meant they would not at some point. Just that they would consider their options and perhaps sound out who else might join them. Atarah buried a smile in Lilya's sweet curls.

"For those of you who belong to my household—I am not presenting this as a choice. My house will serve the Lord and the Lord only. If you do not comply, then I will assume it is because you are no longer willing to accept my authority and serve my family, and so I will immediately send you to the house of someone whose authority you are willing to accept. Am I clear?"

He would sell them—any slave who disobeyed. Perhaps it would seem like a harsh stance to some, but it was a wise one. And she could not imagine any of her fellow servants choosing their ba'als above their loyalty to him. He treated them all with kindness and respect, which was not something they could say of Rimmon, surely.

Lilya fisted a hand in Atarah's hair. "Tarah stay?"

She smiled and kissed the little one's nose. "Of course," she whispered. "I worship none but the Lord."

Naaman glanced at Ramina and then back to the group. "That is all for now. We will depart soon, after I have seen the man of God. Break camp, please."

Ramina slid to Atarah's side, Malak's hand clutched in hers. "I am nervous," she admitted. In a whisper but not like the ones she had always used before that were only air passing through her lips. This whisper had the hum of her voice to it—a voice that had been lifted in song last night with more strength than even Atarah's.

"Why? God has been gracious to your family."

"Yes. So very gracious. But..." She darted a look over her shoulder, at the soldiers. At Ram? "My husband will offer all we have to the prophet, for the Lord. We discussed it all last night. He has given us everything—our health, our family, our future. We would give all back to Him. If He wills us to start fresh, even to leave Syria, then we will. Whatever He asks of us, it is not too great."

Atarah could only stare, agape, for a long moment. They would leave Damascus? Settle...where? *Here?* Was this how Tavi's promise could be kept? Would they return them to their homeland?

She dared not to let the hope take root, not knowing how much it would cost them. She offered Ramina a small smile. "This is quite a sacrifice you are willing to make. No wonder you are nervous."

"It is not the giving that I fear. That, I think, would almost be a relief. It is what the prophet may ask of us that we have not even considered—because surely there will be some cost above what we have already thought of. What if he asks us to dedicate our son to him, like Eli the priest did of Samuel's mother?"

"Ah." Hence the death grip on Malak's hand, she supposed. Atarah shook her head. "I do not know what the Lord may require—but I know that when He asks something of us, He also gives us the strength to accomplish it. And I know, too, that He will not ask for anything that is not to His glory. And it is a privilege to be part of His glory. Part of His story."

Ramina drew in a deep breath, nodded, and turned to where Naaman had paused to await her a few steps away. "I am ready, my husband," she said at a normal, miraculous volume.

He held out an arm to welcome his family—Atarah included, since Lilya was in her arms—to his side. "Come, then. Let us present ourselves to the prophet."

It was a solemn procession to the doors of Elisha's house today. None of the pride of yesterday, none of the lofty expectations. Atarah sensed with every step that her masters were fully prepared for this to be their last walk anywhere as leaders of a grand house. Their postures were of humility, but their steps were sure.

Elisha himself met them at the door today, his staff in his hand and Gehazi a glowering shadow behind him. Atarah made it a point not to meet the gaze of her father's friend. Instead, she kept her eyes trained on the prophet.

He smiled at them. "Did the waters of the Jordan treat you well, my friend?"

Naaman, his most trusted men making a half circle behind him, knelt. "Indeed, now I know that there is no God in all the earth, except in Israel. Now, therefore, please take a gift from your servant."

Elisha lifted his brows. "A gift, you say. One of the songs, perhaps, that I heard you singing in joy last eve?" He glanced briefly at Atarah.

Did he recognize her? Probably—she had surely not changed that much. Had he realized she was here? Quite possibly, given how much else he knew. Would he disapprove?

No—he winked. Actually winked at her, as he had done when she was a child, and gave her half a smile.

Naaman did not lift his head. "All our songs, all our praise, and more besides. I offer all I have with me, my father—my gold, my silver, my spices. Take it all for the Lord."

Elisha's lips twitched again. "God does not need your gold and silver, my son."

"My flocks then—I will have them all driven here as soon as I can."

The prophet chuckled. "The Lord owns the cattle on a thousand hills already."

Now Naaman lifted his head, his face bordering on distraught. "Please, master—if God does not want these things, which I have in abundance, then what can I give to Him? What will you accept?"

With a slow, deliberate movement, Elisha reached out and rested his hand on the top of Naaman's head. "As the Lord lives, before whom I stand, I will receive nothing. You have given already the one thing He requires—your faithful obedience."

"But that cost me nothing!"

"Did it not?" Elisha lifted amused brows. "I think rather it cost you your pride—which is far dearer than any gold or silver.

Rise, my son. Go on your way and take your newfound knowledge with you."

Naaman stood, but he still looked unconvinced. "Surely I can leave something with you, to ease the burden of the coming winter—just a portion of what my soldiers have taken from your land."

Elisha waved him away and turned back to the house. "You have taken only what the Lord turned over to you because of His people's fickle hearts. Use it to serve Him in Damascus—you will have more need of it than I will."

"One moment more, my father, please!"

At the urgency in Naaman's tone, Elisha paused. Turned. Atarah found herself holding her breath.

Naaman gusted his out. "If you will take nothing from me, then perhaps you will grant me something. If I am to return to Damascus, with it will come responsibilities. I would beg of you that you grant your servant two mule-loads of earth, for your servant will no longer offer either burnt offering or sacrifice to other gods but only to the Lord. I would have this visible reminder of the God of Israel, if it is acceptable."

The smile touched Elisha's mouth again. "This is acceptable. And what else is on your mind?"

"I would beg the Lord's pardon." Naaman's hands curled into fists. "When my master the king goes into the temple of Rimmon to worship there and he leans upon my hand and I bow down with him—will the Lord forgive this of me, knowing my heart serves none but Him?"

Elisha's smile tightened, but it did not altogether fade. He looked away for a moment, as if listening to something. Or Someone. And then he nodded. "Go in peace, my son. The Lord knows your heart."

The relief in Naaman's exhale echoed the wonder in her own heart. She had always known the Lord was generous to those who earnestly sought Him, but here was new proof. He asked for nothing, and He would even forgive Naaman's continued presence in the temple of Rimmon?

Atarah craned her head around, searching for Tavi, but he must have been directly behind her—she could not see him from where she stood.

She did, however, spot Gehazi again as she turned, and the dark look in his eyes was like cold water dumped in her face. Elisha might have been generous and forgiving at the urging of God, but clearly his servant did not agree with him.

For a moment, yesterday's distress smothered her heart again, making it difficult to even draw a full breath. She knew Gehazi better than she did Elisha—she had called him *uncle* as a child, had sat in his lap and played with his beard as he told her and Joshua stories of the wonders of God, the tales of Elijah. His own wife had died shortly after they wed, and rather than remarry, he had bound himself in service to the prophets, so Atarah's family had been like his own. She had looked forward to his every visit, had always known she and her siblings were the apples of his eye.

Now he dismissed her with one scathing glare and turned away, striding back into the house with clenched fists and fury bunching his muscles.

She watched him until he vanished. Once he had disappeared behind the door, her breath came more easily again, and the weight that had fallen on her shoulders lifted. Yesterday, his disapproval and censure had seemed as though it was from God Himself. But it was not. It was in direct opposition to Elisha's approval, and of the two of them, only one was the *prophet*.

The burden of Gehazi's hatred was not hers to bear. It would rest on his own shoulders, and she could only pray that he would realize quickly how debilitating it would be and shrug it off. That he would turn that burden over to God and let the sweet waters of forgiveness cleanse him.

Lilya squirmed to be put down, so Atarah placed her on her feet and took her hand instead, shaking her head when the little one tried to pull free. "You must stay by my side, sweet Lilya. We are breaking camp."

After the weeks of travel, the girl knew what that meant— that she had to stay out from underfoot and within sight of Atarah or her mother at all times. Not that knowing it kept her from pouting. "But Lil hungry."

Atarah smiled. "Then we shall go and visit Dafna, shall we?"

No doubt the cook had breakfast ready from the food remaining after last night's feast. They would all be visiting Dafna as they went about their tasks, seeking fortification for what was certain to be a long day of travel back toward Damascus.

Tavi fell into step beside her as they walked back to camp. "I believe all the guards will comply with Naaman's request, given his offer to compensate them for the cost of their charms. They are muttering that our God will probably suffice to watch over them until they can return to their own borders—none seem eager to break away from the caravan and go it alone."

That was good, she supposed. There was always strength in numbers. She smiled up at Tavi, still not quite able to believe in the light of day that this man who had achieved so much so quickly under Naaman's and Seena's tutelage was *hers*. Not just her friend but her future husband. "It is a brave thing our master has done."

Tavi nodded, a gleam in his eye as he watched Naaman and Ramina hurry toward the wagon and chariots. "We can be proud to serve such a master."

A thought that would have struck her as impossible and mad when Naaman had stolen them away from Ramah. But Tavi was right.

Musing more about it would have to wait though. The familiar bustle of breaking camp soon took over her attention, and she dedicated herself to making certain all of Ramina's things were stored in the wagon, that the children were fed and packed and put in the wagon too, and that her own few possessions were stored along with them. Within an hour, the first chariots were leading the way north, back toward Syrian territory.

She could not resist a long look over her shoulder as Elisha's house receded from view. She had slept in the house of a king on this journey. She had seen the evidence of a true miracle. She had seen hatred in the eyes of a man she considered family and acceptance in those of the prophet. She had been given the most precious gift she had ever imagined receiving—Tavi's love.

How unreal it seemed to be leaving, heading back to Aram-Damascus. Everything about their life had changed. And yet... what would be different when they returned home with those donkey loads of Israelite soil? Everything? Or nothing? What if they forgot, when surrounded by the politics of Ben-Hadad's court again, what had happened here?

No. No, they would not forget. They could not—not with Naaman's flesh as smooth and healthy as a babe's now, making him look twenty years younger. Not with Ramina's voice now carrying loud and clear on the breeze.

She faced forward again. She would make it her prayer to remember. Every day, she would lead the children and Ramina in a psalm of thanksgiving for all the Lord had done for them. They would not forget.

They were only an hour outside of Samaria when Tavi, brows furrowed, drew her attention to the road behind them with a jerk of his head. "Someone is coming—chasing after us, it seems."

She craned her head around, seeing in a glance that he was right. A runner was catching up to their rear even now, though he did not look much like a hired courier—his steps were too uneven, as if the run—short for a professional—had taxed him greatly. Which made sense, given the gray of his hair. It was a moment more before her eyes widened with recognition. "Gehazi!"

Tavi sucked in a sharp breath beside her. "I cannot think what he wants."

A dozen beautiful possibilities swam through her mind. Perhaps he had realized his error in judgment and had decided to catch up with them to ask forgiveness. Maybe he meant to assure her that he would tell her parents she lived. Maybe—

Naaman jumped down from the lead chariot, clearly having spotted him as well. He met Gehazi just beside the wagon in which Atarah and Ramina and the children rode. "Is all well?"

Gehazi wheezed for breath. "All is well. My master has sent me, saying, 'Indeed, just now two young men of the sons of the prophets have come to me from the mountains of Ephraim.'"

The mountains of Ephraim? Atarah exchanged raised brows with Tavi. That would be the area near Jezreel, to the north of Samaria. Tavi's family's territory. If students had just arrived at Elisha's home from there, would they not have passed along this very road? But they had seen no one other than a few farmers taking goods to the city.

Though they could have stayed the night in Samaria, she supposed, and set out for Elisha's house at dawn.

Whatever the case, Naaman did not question it. He was nodding, smiling.

Gehazi continued. "My master has said, 'Run to Naaman the Syrian and ask him to give them a talent of silver and two changes of garments.'"

"A talent?" Naaman beamed. "You will take two, one for each of them! It is a pleasure indeed to be allowed to provide for two of the Lord's prophets. Here." He dashed to one of the mules that carried the silver.

Unease skittered up Atarah's spine. She looked at Tavi, who was studying Gehazi with a drawn expression. He no doubt knew the same thing she did—never would Elisha have sent him on such a mission. Once he declared a thing, Elisha did not change his mind. And Elisha had declared that he would take nothing from Naaman's hand.

No, it was not the prophet who had sent Gehazi here.

Naaman waved two of his guards forward. "Ador, Warda— please accompany this man back. It is too much for him alone to carry."

Far too much—that much silver would bow Gehazi's back within two steps. Atarah bit back the sharp words that wanted to spill from her lips in the man's direction. It was greed in his eyes, that was all. Greed and hatred and a desire to take *something* from Naaman, since the Lord and Elisha had spared him what he considered his due punishment.

It was to Naaman's credit that he would give—but it was *not* to Gehazi's that he would take.

Within a few minutes, the three men set off back in the direction from which they had just come, silver and garments weighing them down. Atarah shook her head. Gehazi had not so much as looked her way, and she was glad. He would have seen her disappointment and disgust for him in a glance.

Tavi, jaw tight, faced forward again. "This will not go well for him. The curse he wished upon our master will fall on his head instead."

She did not need to see the fire of the Spirit in his eyes to know he spoke the Truth. She felt it resonating like a deep harmony in her own being.

# CHAPTER FOURTEEN

Tavi jerked awake in the night, his fingers digging into the earth beneath him even as his every sense attempted to enumerate what it was that had disturbed him. A wild animal? An enemy force?

Not since that morning in King Joram's house had he had quite this feeling—as if it was the Spirit's step he had heard, the Spirit's hand that shook him awake, the Spirit's eyes that bade him lift his own.

Darkness still weighed heavily on the camp, no light in the east to brighten the sky or hint at dawn. The only light came from the moon, the stars, and the embers of last night's fire.

They had reached Syrian land yesterday. And it had made his muscles tighten. Not just at the thought of leaving the land of his people but because he had seen—or perhaps sensed?—the reactions of all those around him. Naaman had tensed, had looked over his shoulder, had double-checked the mules with their loads of earth.

But it was the soldiers who had made him remain on alert even as he settled down to sleep as darkness fell. They had all agreed to stay with the party on their return, turning over their charms and talismans and tokens of their gods...but the moment they crossed out of Israelite territory, the moment their homes were within a few days' hard riding, the whispers had begun. The whispers that said it was time to leave the traitor before they could share in his curse, which surely Rimmon would visit upon him now.

Naaman had to have heard them. But he had made no response, given no speech. And when Seena said, "Master?" in that tone of voice that bespoke as much worry as Tavi felt, Naaman had just shaken his head.

Perhaps that was all that had awoken Tavi now—movement of soldiers trying to slip away in the night. If so, he would not stop them, since Naaman clearly did not want him to. Nor did he wish anyone to *think* he was trying to stop them and risk a confrontation that involved a weapon.

He kept his body still, his breathing even, matching the rise and fall of Seena's chest to his right. Only his eyes moved, sending his gaze all about the camp, looking for shadows out of place.

There. To the northward, figures were gathering at the edge of camp, silent and slinking. He could not quite tell how many. A dozen? Hard to say.

More movement, so quiet he could barely make it out, made him tense. Another soldier working his way through the sleeping masses, that was all. And there, to his right, one more.

Perhaps this awareness in his chest was only natural, nothing of the Spirit in it. Or perhaps he was awake merely to make certain they did not attempt to set loose all the horses or otherwise put the company at risk. If they wanted to slip off, so be it, but Tavi would not let their lack of faith in Naaman bring these people he cared most about any harm, not if he could help it.

Slowly, he rolled onto his side so that he could spring up quickly if he had to. He angled his body toward the tent in which Naaman and Ramina, Atarah, and the children were sleeping.

Which was the only reason he saw that other figure, dark as the night and ten times as sneaky, crouching down at the base of the fabric wall and lifting it.

Even in the dark, he recognized him—Ram. He would know him anywhere, given the hours he had studied him, watched him, prayed for wisdom concerning him. And why would Ram be crouching like that, lifting a side of the heavy material? Why would he be wielding something in his hand that glinted in the moonlight?

A knife. Tavi sucked in a breath and rolled the rest of the way onto his stomach, bracing his hands against the ground. He had no idea what exactly he meant to do against Ram, who had many more years of practice in the art of war than he did, but he knew he had to do *something*.

A horse whinnied to the north, loud enough to snag his attention and make others around him stir and shift and roll, though no one sat up. Tavi frowned when hoofbeats then sounded, slowly at first but quickening a moment later. Someone was leaving the camp.

And Ram was bending even lower to the ground, no doubt about to slide beneath the tent wall.

Tavi had to act—now. *Lord, go before me. Help me, guide me. Give me a way to protect them!*

He pushed to his knees and then to his feet even as Ram ducked under the wall. A million terrible images tried to flood Tavi's mind, but he pushed them all away and lunged for the wall, dodging the other sleeping bodies.

Ram's back foot was just disappearing inside. Tavi grabbed it, jerked. An *oof* sounded from inside, along with the thud of a body hitting the ground. Another jerk, harder, and he pulled Ram half back outside.

Another set of hands reached down, and Seena helped him pull Ram the rest of the way out. The man cursed quietly, twisted, kicked at them. He managed to break free and Tavi dropped into the stance that matched Seena's, both of them ready for him to come at them.

Instead, his eyes widened, but they were focused above them, beyond them. Ram scrambled back a few feet and then spun, pure horror on his face, and ran.

Tavi glanced over his shoulder, half expecting to see a dozen more guards on their feet. But no one was there.

"I will make sure they are not stealing all the horses. You follow him," Seena said.

Tavi nodded and slipped through the camp's shadows, chasing after Ram. He was running, swift-footed and silent, toward the north end of camp, where the other figures had been lurking. As he neared them, Ram let out a bird call, which must have been some sort of signal. The shadowy figures began moving, melding with others as they apparently mounted horses.

Tavi increased his speed once he was out of the main group of sleepers, though he took care not to actually catch Ram, who still had his knife gripped in his hand. Moonlight glinted off it with every pump of his arm.

The moment Ram reached his companions, he vaulted onto the back of a horse, which neighed in protest. "Where is Miran? Tell me he did not leave yet!"

"A few minutes ago," one of the other shadows answered quietly.

Ram bit out a curse. "Well, hurry. We must catch him!"

"My lord, you sent him on the fastest horse—we will *never* catch him, you know that!"

Tavi frowned and slipped behind the shield of the wagon. Why would Ram have sent Miran—one of his closest compatriots—anywhere on the fastest horse?

Ram growled and spun his horse northward. "We will have to try."

"You failed then." The other man delivered the sentence evenly, lowly.

It sliced through Tavi's awareness like the knife. This, all this was part of some plan of Ram's. He likely had intended to kill Naaman in his sleep. Perhaps Ramina too—and Atarah and the children. Then flee with those loyal to him and to Rimmon.

Ram hissed something at the man. Tavi could not hear what it was, but it spurred the rest of them to dig their heels into their horses' flanks and fly into the night.

Tavi let his gaze track them as long as he could. And then he stared into the darkness. The fastest horse...that would be Warrior. One of Tavi's favorites, and faster by far than the other stock they had brought with them, the beasts trained to pull chariots or wagons. He would outpace this crew of Ram's without doubt.

The question was, what business was Miran about that Ram's failure would make it critical he halt?

Atarah knew the moment they came within sight of Damascus that something was wrong—and she was not the only one. Ramina's eyes narrowed. Naaman sucked in a startled breath. Seena muttered a few words that probably should not have been said in the company of women or children.

The house, on the outer wall of the city as it was, was before them. That same house, which they had shut up for the duration of their absence and left under guard, now had servants scurrying about it, on the rooftop and passing into and out of the courtyard, and a strange standard flapping in the wind where Naaman's flag usually flew.

Strange but not unfamiliar.

"Lebario." Ramina spat her uncle's name like a curse and spun on the wagon's seat to face her husband.

"Easy, my love." Naaman held up a hand to halt the procession, reining in his own chariot and just staring ahead at the house for a long moment. He must be feeling something, but whatever it was, it did not show on his face. He simply jumped down and held up his arms to Malak, who was eager to get out of the wagon. "Set up camp!" he yelled to his men. "Here, outside the walls. You who are soldiers—if you would grant me a few more hours of your time?"

It was what he always did with his army when they returned, or at least with what they brought back with them. But this time, the plan had been for all the soldiers to report directly back to their places, and for the household to go immediately into the house and unpack while Naaman presented himself to the king. He had gone over this plan just a few hours ago, when they had broken camp that morning.

The captain of the soldiers saluted. "We are at your disposal, my lord."

Atarah climbed down from the wagon with the others, gladly accepting Tavi's hand in assistance. But her gaze drifted back to the house and that blue banner snapping in the wind where Naaman's red should have been. "What have they done, do you think?"

Tavi shook his head. "Nothing good."

"I knew it." Ramina, already on the ground, rubbed a hand over the bulge of her coming child, eyes blazing. "I knew they would try something in Naaman's absence. They have always wanted what was his, always thought my uncle should have been given the rewards Naaman received. But to take it forcibly—I cannot believe they convinced the king to allow this!"

"We do not know that they did." Naaman had lifted Lilya into his arms but still had a hand free to rub a soothing circle on his wife's back. "I will send a messenger to the king, telling him we are here."

"A messenger?" Ramina frowned. "He will expect you to go yourself, as we discussed."

"Yes. But if Lebario has turned his head away from me, it could be suicide to walk into his throne room. If he wishes to see me, it will be out here, in open territory. If I am no longer welcome in his city, then we will simply leave. But I will present neither myself nor my family for slaughter."

Seena slid up to them too. "I wonder if this has something to do with Ram's departure when we reached Aram."

Tavi drew in a long breath. "It very well could. Perhaps he did not dare to reenter Damascus with us, given whatever is going on here."

Atarah eased up close to Tavi's side, needing the comfort his presence brought her. She had always known that Naaman's enemies could mean danger to the family, yes. But somehow it had always seemed distant, a mere possibility, especially after his healing. The Lord surely would not have delivered him from leprosy only to deliver him into the hands of Lebario the moment he got home.

But then, Elisha had said Naaman would have more need of his wealth than the schools did—perhaps this was what he had meant. Perhaps Naaman would have to move his family elsewhere, purchase property somewhere else, build a new home. She hated the thought of Lebario and Ram winning, but perhaps that would be the easier path. Let them have Ben-Hadad and Damascus and just go somewhere they could live and worship in peace.

Wherever that might be.

"Why can we not go home, Mother?" Malak asked, wrapping an arm around Ramina's leg.

The mistress sighed and smoothed his hair back from his face. "It would seem that Uncle Lebario and Aunt Izla are staying in our house right now. But we have become experts at finding our ease in a camp, have we not?"

Malak's quivering lip disagreed.

So did Ramina's eyes, suddenly tired. She had been musing all morning about her anticipation of a hot bath. After months on the road, Atarah certainly felt as though she had dust in her very pores. Such luxuries would apparently have to wait though.

What they needed was a distraction. She clapped her hands, pasting a bright smile on her face. "I know how we shall pass the time. I have been composing a song, and I need help finishing it."

Malak peeked up at her, dubious. "I thought David wrote all the songs."

"All the songs in the whole world?" She laughed. "No. Some of my favorites, but there are many psalms besides his, and many more waiting to be written. Would you help me?"

Lilya lunged for the ground. "Lil help! Lil sing!"

"I think we will need some instruments too. Malak, would you prefer the tambourine today or a drum?"

Just the choice to convince him to let go of his mother's leg. "Both!"

She laughed. "Both? But you have only two hands."

"I can switch."

"Very good then." With a wink for her mistress, she led the children to the back of the wagon again and dug around until she could pull out the crate with their instruments. She was teaching Malak how to play both the lyre and the psaltery, but it was slow going, and he grew bored of it quickly. Lessons had helped pass some of the time during their travels, but percussion was much more to the four-year-old's current tastes when it came time to actually sing together.

Tavi hefted the crate of instruments down for her, a grin in his eyes. "You did not tell me you were writing your own songs now, beloved."

Her cheeks warmed. "One song, and it is unfinished. And probably no good anyway. I am certainly no David."

He handed her the psaltery she thought of as her own, though it belonged, of course, to Ramina. "You do not need to be David. You need only to be you. To share the words of praise God puts on your heart. Do so faithfully, to the best of your ability, and it will be good and pleasing in His sight."

She took the instrument with a self-conscious smile. "A reminder I needed. Thank you, Tavi."

They passed the next hour with music and laughter. She taught the children and Ramina what she had thus far of her song, all about finding restoration from the Lord in His waters, of His faithfulness even in the desert sands. Their suggestions for finishing the last stanza were more humorous than serious, but she had not honestly expected them to help her finish. She had simply known setting their minds to it would distract them from that blue standard snapping above them and the fact that they were camping outside their own walls instead of settling back within them.

And singing a reminder of Yahweh's faithfulness settled her own spirit too. He was greater than Lebario. Greater than Ram. Greater than Ben-Hadad. He could flick their problems aside if He so chose—and if not, then the difficulty would be for His glory. She sang that promise in a harmony that wrapped around Ramina's melody, filling the skies above them.

"Beautiful, ladies."

Ramina scrambled to her feet, eyes wide, only to dip low again. "My king!"

What? Atarah bowed too, not even daring to look up. She had seen the king before, of course, when he came to dine at Naaman's table, but never this close. And he had never addressed her, even along with someone else.

Ben-Hadad waved a hand. "At ease, my dear. But what is this I hear? Your voice! It has been restored?"

Ramina kept her head down. "By the grace of God, yes."

"Excellent. You can sing for me again at my next feast, then. And perhaps your maid with you—she has a remarkable voice."

Ramina reached back and squeezed Atarah's hand. "The fairest voice in all the land, my king. And we would be honored to sing for you."

*Honored* was not the word that sprang immediately to Atarah's mind, but she did not imagine that *terrified* was quite the picture her mistress would want to portray.

Thankfully, Naaman strode up then, commanding the king's attention. "My lord and king, greetings!"

"Greetings, Naaman." Even in those two words, Ben-Hadad sounded bemused. "Happy I am to see your safe return—though I am confused as to why you did not come and present yourself as you usually do."

Naaman bowed deeply, though quickly. Once he straightened, Ramina edged back, nudging Atarah with her. The children scurried out of the way too, back toward the wagon.

Perhaps they ought to make themselves scarce as well, but curiosity made Atarah hope they might stay instead. And apparently Ramina had the same thought, because she retreated only a few steps before tugging Atarah to a halt.

"I pray you will forgive me if I have caused any offense," Naaman said, his voice humble to match his stance. "I was uncertain of our reception."

The king frowned. "This prophet of Israel failed, then? Has your leprosy spread?"

"On the contrary." Naaman tossed aside the cloak that had been covering his arms against the chill and presented his forearm. "My skin has been restored as new."

"Amazing!" Ben-Hadad lurched forward for a closer look, bending close to inspect the flesh. "Did you not also have a scar on this arm, from the first raid you led?"

"I did. As you see, the Lord's healing is complete."

With a quiet laugh, the king straightened. "Amazing indeed—though I must then ask again why you would fear what kind of reception you would receive. I have been eagerly awaiting your return these months."

"I am relieved to hear it."

They would *all* be relieved, as Atarah was. If Naaman was still in Ben-Hadad's favor, then perhaps they may yet find peace here.

"But," her master continued, turning toward the house and motioning toward the flag, "you can perhaps understand my confusion upon returning and finding another man's household in my house. What could I think, but that you had ordered my belongings given to him? Because surely he would not be so bold otherwise."

"He? He who?" The king squinted at the standard, but his eyesight must not have been sharp enough anymore to let him see it clearly.

"Lebario, my lord."

The king actually took a step back in surprise. "Lebario? But that—there must be some misunderstanding. He is your wife's uncle. Perhaps he has merely sent his servants to your house to prepare it for your arrival."

And instructed them to fly *his* banner? Atarah pressed her lips together to keep from pointing out the obvious flaw in the king's logic.

Naaman refrained as well, though his eyes said he found the explanation utterly unconvincing.

Ben-Hadad sighed. "Or perhaps he received a false report of how your journey went and thought you would not be returning. That hardly explains his presence there when no one has breathed a word of any of this to me, but I am certain there is a reasonable explanation. Come, we shall discover what it is."

Atarah looked at her mistress, brows raised. "Well, he will quickly set things to rights, I imagine," she whispered.

Ramina shook her head. "Even if he does, my aunt and uncle will never forgive it." She spun to the wagon, where the children were playing, Dafna watching over them. After a quick request that she continue doing so for a few minutes more, Ramina took Atarah's hand and hurried them after Naaman and Ben-Hadad, who had already started for the house.

The king had arrived with a large retinue of soldiers, and several of them led the way to the doors, clearing any passersby from the path. As Atarah kept pace with Ramina, she had to wonder what had become of the servants they had left in charge of the place—had they simply been overwhelmed by the arrival of Lebario's people and stepped aside in the interest of peace? Had they been bribed to go along with it? Or, worst possibility of all, had they been silenced for any objections they made?

She drew forward the image of the steward and his family, praying as she walked that they were well.

By the time they reached the front entrance, the soldiers had already made their presence known and were even then leading Lebario and his wife from the house. Neither was going quietly, but upon spotting the king and Naaman, their bluster came to an abrupt halt. Lebario washed pale. Then pasted a too-bright smile onto his face. "Nephew! Praise to the gods, you are well! I thought you had been killed."

Naaman folded his arms across his chest—displaying, if Lebario cared to look, his restored skin. "And why, Uncle, would you have thought that, I wonder?"

Lebario spread his hands wide. "That is what the message our son sent us said. Is it not, Izla?"

Atarah was glad for the many soldiers around, given the dark look Izla wore. Perhaps it was aimed at her husband for seemingly offering their son up for the king's displeasure, but she suspected it was more for the rest of them. "Indeed," she muttered.

"How curious." Naaman's voice was flat as the plains. "Clearly he was…mistaken. Or someone sent a false message to you. A jest, no doubt."

"Yes! A jest." The king seemed to seize that excuse with both hands. "One in poor taste, to be sure, but only a jest. One we will put behind us. Obviously, and obviously to your joy, your nephew and niece have returned. So we will thank you for preparing their house for them…" The king shot a glance up at the banner waving above the door, then sent a pointed, reproachful look at Lebario. "And we will step out of your way while you repair back to your own lodgings. Unless you have some problem with the grand house I gave you permission to occupy?"

Lebario's cheeks flushed. "No problem at all, my lord. We were only attempting to make certain everything was safe for my niece and her children, on the hope that they had escaped the fate we thought had befallen her husband." Then his gaze moved to Naaman. "Where is my son? We will clear up this miscommunication with him at once."

Naaman's only movement was a lift of his brow. "A fine question. He and two dozen others abandoned us as soon as we crossed into Syrian territory. I have a feeling you will see him before I do."

Ben-Hadad turned away. "Well, when he turns up, I would like to see him too, to discuss our raiding campaign for the spring. General, I will need your insights too, of course, though I think you have earned a season of rest after your travels."

Atarah's heart stuttered at the mention of raids. Into Israel's lands again, or would they be striking at some other neighbor? Either way, she was glad her master would not be expected to lead any of the raiding parties this time.

And she wondered why the king was so willing to overlook what was obviously a nefarious deception on Ram's part. How could he be so willfully blind to Ram's obvious machinations?

Lebario and his wife stepped back inside to issue a few orders to someone, and then they exited the house fully. Izla surged forward to wrap Ramina in an embrace. "My darling niece! I am so relieved you are well and home again!"

Ramina stood stiffly in her arms. "Thank you, Aunt."

Atarah was near enough to hear the next words the woman hissed in her ear though. "Enjoy your homecoming while it lasts—you will pay for this embarrassment."

Ramina said nothing, just lifted her chin. Then the moment Izla moved away enough to allow it, she rested her hand over her growing stomach.

Their homecoming was sure to be many things—but peaceful was definitely not among them.

# CHAPTER FIFTEEN

*Four Months Later*

Morning dew dampened the carefully tended earth, bringing the lingering scents of home to Atarah's nose. Eyes closed, she breathed it in, smiling at the feel of the sun's first rays upon her face. She faced south, toward home, humming a little slip of melody as she let the words of her prayer fade into heaven.

Beside her, Tavi drew in a long breath, held it, and then let it slowly out before saying, "Amen."

"Amen." She opened her eyes and smiled over at him. They had been doing this for months now, ever since Naaman had set up this little island of Israel on the roof, and she had begun to wonder how she had ever started a day otherwise. There was nothing quite like Tavi, words of praise, earnest beseeching for what they needed, and the first breath of dawn.

He stood and held out a hand to help her to do the same. Then raised it, kissed it, and stared long into her eyes. "We are one day closer to you being my wife," he whispered.

She chuckled. He said something similar nearly every morning, and it always lit a spark of longing in her heart. Thus far, though, neither of them had felt those sparks fan into a blaze that demanded they take action and ask Naaman for his approval of a match. They would walk the course they had agreed upon at Elisha's house. They would trust that the day would come and know that every new dawn brought them closer to it. She pulled his hand toward her so she could return the kiss. "One day closer. Be careful today, beloved."

A warning as familiar as his promise but one she felt necessary to repeat daily. He was the one swinging swords in the arena every day and then walking the streets of Damascus with the master, lingering outside the temple of Rimmon. Danger was his constant shadow, and she had no desire to lose him before their betrothal was even official. Or ever.

"As always." He touched his forehead to hers and then pulled away. "We had better go in. The mistress will need you, and I am due on the training field soon."

She nodded and turned with him toward the stairs.

"Atarah?" Ramina's voice drifted up to them, making Atarah dash to her. The mistress had paused before her head crested the wall, rubbing a hand over her belly.

"My lady! Why are you up so early? Is everything well? The baby?"

Ramina wrinkled her nose. "Making me uncomfortable, but that is all. I could not sleep another minute so thought I would find you. I have not interrupted your prayers, have I?"

"I just finished. Would you like to come up, or should I come down?"

The lady considered for a moment. "Down. I think breakfast will soon be in order. Good morning, Tavi." She could not possibly see him from where she stood, but she grinned as she called out the greeting anyway.

Tavi came up behind Atarah. "Good morning, my lady. Can I get anything for you?"

"No, no." Putting a hand to the wall to steady herself, Ramina turned and began a slow descent of the steep stairs. By their best guess, she had another three or four weeks before the babe was due to arrive, but to look at her, one would think her labor pains could come upon her at any moment. She made it a point to keep moving as much as possible, but the stairs to the roof were growing increasingly troublesome for her.

Atarah hovered close behind her, so that she could reach out and grab her elbow if she stumbled. Once they were all safely on solid ground, Tavi bade them farewell and went off in search of his own breakfast.

Ramina headed for her airy receiving chamber, sending Atarah a smirk. "You two have been spending more time than ever together."

"Have we?" Atarah plumped a pillow for her mistress to recline against. "What are you hungry for this morning? A fruit plate? Yogurt? Bread and cheese?"

"It all sounds lovely, so whatever Dafna has ready—but do not think you can change the subject so easily." Wiggling her brows, Ramina patted the cushion next to her. "Sit. We so rarely have time before the children get up, as late as I have been these days, and with Malak refusing to nap, we never get time to talk."

Atarah made herself comfortable on the cushion, grinning back. "If your stomach starts talking as loudly as your mouth, you have only yourself to blame."

The novelty of hearing her mistress's voice still struck her at odd moments. And sometimes when she laughed, Atarah saw a look of grateful adoration pass over Naaman's face. It had, after all, been her injury that introduced them. He had never really heard her voice, not until Yahweh healed her.

She laughed now and rubbed at a lump that moved across her stomach. An elbow? A tiny foot? Atarah found it fascinating to watch that new life stretching itself out in her friend's stomach. And she prayed that, if the Lord willed, her own wedding would come soon enough that she would not be too old to bear Tavi children. She wanted to experience this miracle for herself someday, even if years in the future. If it took decades, though, then so be it—she would just trust that the Lord could use even an aged womb, as He had Sarah's, if He wanted Tavi to have heirs.

"Now." Eyes twinkling, Ramina lifted her brows. "When are you going to tell me what changed between you on our journey? I have been very patient, I think."

Atarah's cheeks burned. "What makes you think anything has changed?"

Ramina laughed. "Atarah, please. I have eyes, have I not? You were always close, but there is something new, and it is ever growing. And if it matters at all, you have my full approval. I cannot think of a young man more deserving of you."

The blush felt as though it had spread over her whole face and down her neck too. "In that we can agree. Tavi is more than I ever dreamed a man could be." He had the wisdom of her father, the faith of Elisha, the daring of Naaman, the skill of Seena—and a heart for her alone.

"So then?" Ramina poked her in the ribs. "When are you going to speak to my husband?"

And this was why she had never dared to mention the shift in her relationship with Tavi. She shrugged. "We are in no hurry to wed, my lady. Tavi is so deep in his studies again since we returned, and with this new little one coming so soon... Besides, it has been lovely to simply enjoy each other's company."

"I can take a hint—but you have to at least tell me what happened in Israel. Indulge me that far, will you not?"

Though Atarah sighed, a giggle chased it. "All right."

She did not give her the full story, of course—she had no desire to explain Gehazi's hatred of the Syrians and his insistence that Atarah was a traitor. But she told her of Tavi finding her by the stream and admitting that he had spoken to her father about marrying her. Of her wonder. Of that first beautiful kiss.

Ramina's eyes were wide through the telling. "You mean—all these years? Tavi practically volunteered for slavery to come with you, to protect you?" She clasped her hands over her heart. "That is the sweetest thing I have ever heard!"

Atarah could only catch her lip between her teeth and nod.

"Then I am all the more confused as to why you are in so little a hurry. He has already been waiting years for you."

Quick footsteps approaching the door saved her from answering, though when the steward burst in, panting from exertion, her relief was short-lived. "Mistress! The king—the king is coming. Here. Now—he will be here in ten minutes, his runner said."

"What?" Blanching, Ramina pushed herself forward, holding out a hand to Atarah so she could help her to her feet. "Why on earth would the king be coming here at this hour? Where is my husband?"

"Out in the barracks already, but someone is fetching him. Dafna is putting together all the food she has prepared. But the ba'al, my lady..."

They had removed it from the house as their first order of business upon returning and thus far had never had to fear the king noting its absence—he had come to dine with them once, but the evening had been so fair that they had taken the meal outside. And otherwise, the family had been invited to the palace instead.

Ramina sucked in a breath. "There is no help for that. He will notice or he will not, and if he does, we will simply explain the truth to him. It was inevitable that this day would come. But I am more concerned over what *else* is bringing him here. So far as I know, Ben-Hadad never leaves the palace before noon."

Atarah squeezed the hand she still held. "We will see soon enough."

Perhaps her words, quiet as they were, instilled a bit of calm in her mistress. Or perhaps the peace of the Lord did that. She visibly stilled, squeezing Atarah's fingers back. "You must come with me, Atarah. Bring your instruments. If my husband cannot be found quickly enough, we will have to entertain him."

She turned to the steward. "Please instruct your daughter to tend the children when they awake."

"Of course, my lady."

Atarah darted for her instruments while the man disappeared. "You must dress, my lady, quickly." Ramina still wore the rumpled tunic she had slept in, as was her usual habit until after she had broken her fast.

Though what exactly was appropriate attire for entertaining a king before the sun had fully crested the hills?

Her mistress squeaked a bit and dashed toward her bed chamber as quickly as her awkward stomach would allow. "There is no time to do more than brush my hair, I daresay."

After stowing the instruments by the door for easy grabbing on their way out, Atarah hurried after Ramina and went directly to her clothing. "Here." She pulled out the lady's favorite linen tunic, loose enough to fit comfortably now, and then reached for the finely woven overdress in blue, with a few threads of precious purple visible, which she usually reserved for special occasions.

This surely classified.

The moment Ramina emerged from behind her screen, Atarah was ready with the hairbrush. She tackled the dark tresses, still tangled from sleep, while the lady considered a dozen jewelry options before deciding on a simple bangle and the wide gold collar Naaman had given her before their trip to Israel.

No one had shouted up yet that Ben-Hadad was there, so Atarah whipped the lady's hair into a quick braid. "There. Good enough."

And just in time, given the cry from the door. Without even the leisure to exchange a harried glance, they both rushed downstairs, Ramina using the wall to steady herself and Atarah carrying her psaltery.

They had just taken up their places in the receiving chamber when Ben-Hadad walked in, agitation in his every jerky movement.

"My king." Ramina bowed. Atarah held her arm to steady her and help her straighten again. "What an honor to welcome you to my home this morning. Please, sit down. Enjoy some of Dafna's famous fig cakes."

Atarah had not even had the chance to notice that the low table had been covered with dishes of delicious-looking food. Dafna had been cooking relentlessly in recent days, trying to anticipate what delicacy Ramina might be craving. Her overeagerness had certainly served them all well today.

"Thank you, Ramina, but it is your husband I seek. Is he at home?"

Though she might have looked frantic on her way down the stairs, Ramina was the figure of graceful calm now. She held out a hand to the best chaise. "He will be in directly, my lord. Being as diligent a commander as you know he is, he was already at the barracks inspecting his soldiers. You might as well sit to await him. Perhaps a cup of fresh juice? Dafna just squeezed it this morning."

At her discreet nod, Atarah took her cue to pick up her instrument. She positioned herself on her stool in the corner of the room, where she was usually stationed when they had guests. Here, no one would really notice her, but she could weave a tapestry of melody to drape the room.

As she always did, she chose one of the songs she had grown up with, plucking out each note without need for thought. Her fingers knew them all, as did her throat. A hum worked its way out too, though she kept herself from singing the words. Had it only been the family, she would have, but the king probably would not care to hear about David's exploits put to music.

Besides, while humming, she could still listen as Ramina worked her own skills, convincing the king to relax and accept a plate filled with Dafna's finest. He was just polishing off his second date cake and actually laughing at Ramina's story of the children's latest adventure, when Naaman strode in.

The master executed a quick bow. "Forgive me for keeping you waiting, my king—though I see my lovely wife has made sure your wait was pleasant."

"As always, my friend." Ben-Hadad licked the sweet, sticky juice from his fingers and set the plate down. "But please, join me. I seek your input on a most urgent matter."

Atarah's first thought was *Ram*. He had eventually shown up back in Damascus, though only a month ago. But he had returned with spoils enough from a raid on Mari—carried out by the other soldiers he had pilfered from Naaman's retinue— that the king had not batted a lash at his unauthorized absence. Nor had anyone brought up the lie he had sent his parents about Naaman, so far as she knew.

It was bound to resurface at some point, though. If she had learned anything about royal politics since she arrived in

Damascus, it was that even the smallest slight was cataloged and stored up for later use. It might be glossed over for a time, but it would come back to bite one at the least opportune moment.

The master sat, accepting with a smile the cup of fruit juice that Ramina passed him. "I am at your service, my king."

Ben-Hadad sat forward, bracing his elbows against his legs. "While I realize I have had you focusing largely on the strategy we should take if the treaty with Irhuleni should fall through, you are surely aware that the raids on the Hebrew territory have continued."

Naaman took a sip of his juice. His hand did not shake, nor did his fingers tighten around his chalice, but she knew how torn her master's heart was on this matter. He and Ramina had spoken of it in hushed tones when there was no one but her or Tavi or Seena around to overhear. "I am aware, yes. Though I have not heard the reports on how they have gone, nor seen the raiders returning with their spoils."

"Because there have *been* no spoils!" The king punctuated his shout with the hammer of a fist upon the table, making the pottery rattle.

It took every bit of calm Atarah possessed to keep her music light and even.

Naaman frowned. "No spoils? At all?"

"None." Now the king stood, clearly agitated. "I have planned each excursion carefully, as always. But each time I send the men in, that blasted Joram has moved his army into place to stop them! It has happened time and time again since you returned."

The master's frown only deepened. "How many times?"

The king snorted. "Not just once or twice. Lebario is right, there is only one possible explanation—someone in the court is for Israel."

*Lebario.* It took no great wisdom to know in which direction he would have been pointing his finger. Only one of the king's men had a clear tie to Israel, the sort that might shift his loyalties.

Naaman set his cup calmly onto the table. "Will you look me in the eye and accuse me of betraying you, my king? Have I not served at your side these twenty years? Have I ever once given you cause to doubt me?"

For a moment, she feared Ben-Hadad would take his challenge and do just that—accuse him of being a traitor. Instead, he sighed. "You have been one of my truest friends, Naaman. But *someone* is feeding Joram information. If not you, then who? Which of my men has put a knife in my back?"

"None, my lord, O king." Naaman stood too. And stretched out his once-leprous arm. "But are you forgetting? There is a prophet in Israel capable of miracles. A man who knew my nature without ever having met me. The prophet Elisha could tell the king of Israel the words that you speak in your own bedroom. Do you think the movements of your troops are secret from him?"

"The prophet." Though Atarah could not see the king's face now, he spoke the word darkly. "You mean to tell me that the man who healed you is the one foiling my every move now?"

"I am telling you that the Lord of Hosts shares many secrets with this man. I cannot say he *did* tell his king of your movements, but I know without question that he *could* have."

For a long moment, neither of the men said anything—they just stared at each other. Ramina caught Atarah's eye, conveying in a single look all the worry mounting in her chest. A worry Atarah well understood. This could be it, the last moment they had as free people in Damascus. Ben-Hadad could declare them all traitors, seize the house and the slaves, have Naaman and his family put to death. There was none to stop him, save God.

*Lord my God, my Savior, my Deliverer! Protect these faithful hearts!*

At length, the king huffed out a breath. "Lebario said you would accuse his son of being the spy, with all the time he was gone."

Naaman lifted his brows. "I think Ram is capable of many things, given his ambition—but he cannot be in two places at once. And he was on our eastern border these months, not our southern. I have verified that from several of my men who went with him."

"You do not like him, either of them."

Naaman tilted his head. "This is true. I have little respect for a man who would murder his cousin simply because she refused to pour him another chalice of wine or for the father who would encourage avarice and violence above honor and self-restraint. But I would never cast aspersions their way. I would never try to tarnish them in your eyes. My quarrels with them are my own, personal."

And surely the king was wise enough to see the contrast he painted between them. Naaman would not lie to ruin them, but they would do it to him. Naaman would never try to harm them in court, but they had been doing so tirelessly.

If either of their words could be trusted above the other, there should be no contest.

Ben-Hadad nodded, some of his agitation fading. No, solidifying. Turning to determination. "Never once have you advised me for your own gain or breathed a dishonest word in my hearing, Naaman. So I will not doubt you now. Which means there is only one possible course of action."

Naaman looked far from comforted by the pronouncement. "And what is that?"

"I must capture this prophet. Elisha."

# CHAPTER SIXTEEN

They would not succeed. They *could* not succeed. But even knowing that there was no possible way under heaven that Yahweh would allow the Syrian army to capture His prophet, Tavi felt sick even thinking about it.

He stood absolutely still against the wall in the kitchen, where Naaman had gathered a handful of the servants and explained the situation in hushed tones during the midday meal. There was a weight to the master's word. A heaviness. A burden that Tavi well understood.

Could they really just sit back and do nothing to help? Yet if they tried, they would prove to the king that Naaman and his household could *not* be trusted.

More, the whole reason for this new mission was that Elisha had been foiling the army at every turn. He would do so again this time.

Sometimes though, it was such a challenge for Tavi to think with his faith instead of his fears.

Dafna pressed a hand to her bosom in dismay. "Tell me he did not ask you to lead this expedition, master. Please, tell me he does not mean to test your loyalty in this way."

Tavi's throat went dry, and he glanced down at Atarah, who stood beside him. She had been there that morning, she had heard all the king said. Surely if he had uttered such words, she would have told him. Warned him.

Naaman shook his head. "No, he is adamant, praise be to God, that I am most needed here, to plan the possible attack on Assyria. He has put Ram in charge of it."

A dozen tongues hissed their opinion of that, Tavi's among them. He had been far happier when that man was nowhere in sight. Though he ought to have known a viper like him was only slithering into position for a new strike.

Though if Naaman's role would not change and there was nothing they could do to stop Ram, why had he gathered them here?

And now that he paused to consider it, Tavi looked at the handpicked servants in this room and frowned to realize that though they were from the house, the stables, the sheepfolds, and the guards' barracks, there was one thing they all had in common—they were Hebrews. "Master...why have you called us here? Us, in particular?"

Naaman looked around at them all before meeting Tavi's eye. "As usual, you see to the heart of the matter, Tavi." Bracing himself against the table, Naaman drew in a deep breath. "You have all become family to me—not just because you are part of my household but because we now serve the same God. You know that I want only the best for you."

Tavi nodded along with the others, his hand reaching blindly for Atarah's.

Naaman drew in a long breath. "There is a logic to Lebario's case against me. Of all the houses in Syria, mine is the one with a new but strong tie to Israel. Of all the soldiers in Syria, I am the one who owes a debt to Elisha." He paused, swallowed. "Of all the Hebrew slaves in Syria, mine are the ones whom I recently took back into their homeland."

Half a dozen objections and assurances sprang up, but Naaman silenced them with a lifted hand. "I am not saying any of you did anything that the king would find suspicious. I am merely saying that when Ram's forces fail, Lebario will point all the more wildly at us. I can defend myself because of my relationship with the king. But if he demands any of *you* answer for these supposed crimes..." He shook his head. "You know the law. The king could take any of you, at any moment, and he would owe me only the price of your purchase. I cannot protect you, my friends."

Atarah gripped Tavi's hand with both of hers. "What are you planning, my father?" she asked softly.

Naaman studied each of them in turn. Tavi could not know what Naaman saw when he looked upon the others—but Tavi knew what he felt when this man held his gaze. That God had smiled on him indeed when He led this general twice into his path. That these three years in captivity had equipped him for life in ways nothing else could have. That it was an honor to know him, a blessing to have played a role in his healing, a privilege to protect his family.

That this man, this general whose orders had destroyed everything he once thought he wanted, had become his father.

"I am setting you all free," Naaman said quietly after he had finished his perusal of them all. "I have spent the morning drawing up the contracts granting you legal freedom in Aram-Damascus—though of course, they will be unneeded when you return to Israel."

"Return?" Dafna fanned her face with her hand. "How, my lord? How can we leave you for a place that has not been home for some of us for decades?"

With a gentle smile, Naaman reached out and rested a hand on the cook's shoulder. "You will find a home with each other if you cannot locate your family. I will provide enough for you all to build new lives for yourselves. And Tavi will lead you back."

He said it so easily, effortlessly, as if they had discussed this and Tavi had assured him he was up for the challenge.

They had not. And he was none too sure he was. His throat went dry, and he might have slid to the floor in a heap of fears had Atarah's fingers not anchored him.

*Freedom.* He was handing them their freedom and giving them permission—nay, *ordering* them—to return home. Home to Israel. Home to Ramah. Home to Atarah's family and the covenant waiting to be made.

He nodded his agreement. "I would be honored."

"Trust him to guide you safely and to protect you." Naaman looked over, straight into his eyes again. "There is no one into whose hands I could ever be more comfortable putting you all."

Atarah rubbed her hand over his wrist. "When?"

The master's gaze shifted to her. "At first light tomorrow. Before Lebario has any time to act against you."

Though she had known she would have to leave this family someday if ever they were to return to hers as Tavi had said they would do, Atarah had not once thought it would happen so soon. Or imagined that the tears would be coursing down her cheeks so steadily as she clung to the mistress who had become her friend. "I cannot believe this is goodbye."

Ramina held her as if she never meant to let her go. "You are the sister of my heart." Perhaps she meant to say more, but a sob interrupted her.

Atarah needed no other words anyway. Those she would treasure forever. "I will not even know whether this new babe is a boy or a girl!"

"I will send you a letter. Somehow." Pulling away a little, Ramina wiped her cheeks. "To the School of the Sons of the Prophets in Ramah. You will find your way there, Atarah. You will find your way home."

She could only nod. She trusted that Tavi could lead them there safely. "I will. And...and if ever you must leave too, you are welcome there with my family. Any time. Please know that."

Ramina gave her a watery smile. "Thank you. Though..." She glanced across the room, to where Naaman and Tavi had their heads together, going over the plan. She dropped her voice to her old whisper. "Naaman says that he intends to retire from this life and take us to his family's vineyard, if the king will grant him permission. It will be a quieter life. A safer one. And one far removed from court intrigue."

"Good." Atarah gripped her friend's hand and squeezed it. "That will be a better life for you all. You will be able to worship the Lord in peace."

Ramina nodded. "I pray the king will not object. I think he may insist we stay here for this campaign he is planning against Assyria, but after that…"

"Yes. After that, a new life."

*A new life.* As she said the words, she heard the melody of them in her head. A perfect ending to the song she had been working on these six months. A perfect summary of what the Lord gave all who came to Him.

He was the one who turned old men into fathers of nations. Slaves into second in command. Murderers into prophets. Shepherds into kings. He was the Lord who took their broken pieces and made them whole, took their broken dreams and gave them something greater than they ever could have imagined.

She leaned in for one more hug. "I will miss you and the children."

"And we you. But we are better for having known you, Atarah."

"As am I." She pulled away this time with a sigh, itching to slip back into the children's room one last time. But they were asleep, and she had already told them goodbye, explaining that it was time she returned to her own abba and imma. She had kissed them, had sung them each a song just for them, and had whispered in their ears, "Trust always in Yahweh. He who parted the Red Sea could reunite us one day, if He wills it."

They would grow up, and they would likely forget the handmaid who had served them when they were so small. But they would remember the Lord, thanks to the instruction of their parents. That was what mattered.

On the other side of the room, Tavi and Naaman straightened.

"Just be aware at all times that Ram's soldiers could be on a similar route," Naaman said, rolling up the parchment and handing it to Tavi. "Your group is small, so it will be easy for you to take cover and remain unseen. His force will be large and loud—surprise is not what they are trying to achieve."

Atarah's stomach tied itself in a few knots at the thought of running into Ram or any of his soldiers. She had a feeling that he would not care a whit about those papers saying they were free—he would not even wait to see them. If he spotted them, he would order them killed.

But the Lord would be their protector. He had not led them this far just to turn them over to their enemy on the brink of returning home. She had to believe that.

Tavi tucked the scroll into a bag that already had several others in it—he would be returning to Israel wealthy in writings if nothing else.

"Here." Naaman next pulled forward a large box with an intricate-looking lock. "Grab those sacks of grain there, if you would."

Atarah had wondered at their presence in this room, especially when she had peeked inside and saw that weevils had found their way into the grain. After wrinkling her nose in disgust, she had been happy to turn away from the bags and focus upon the children and Ramina. Now, though, she moved to help Tavi carry them toward the box.

"It would look odd if a dozen Hebrews were spotted with bags clinking with coins." Naaman opened the box, revealing gold and silver in neat stacks. More of it than she had ever seen at once in her life. "And I cannot exactly send you with guards enough to ward off bandits. But no one will be interested in spoiled grain." He scooped up a handful of coins and dropped them into the nearest bag, then shook it until the coins worked their way through the grain and insects.

At Naaman's gesture, Tavi reached into the chest to pull out another handful of coins, though he looked adorably uncertain as he did so. "I do not know how much, my lord."

"All of it." At Tavi's indrawn breath, Naaman chuckled. "Do not fret, my son. This is hardly my whole fortune. We will divide this between the bags, and when you arrive in Israel, you give one bag to each person."

A bag each? That would be enough for anyone to buy a vineyard or an orchard or a shop or a herd or...anything they wanted. To *be* anything they wanted. Atarah shook her head. "You are too generous, my lord."

"It is wealth taken from your land, either directly or indirectly. Please allow me to repay it in some small part—to give back to those faithful to the Lord our God."

Elisha had argued, but Atarah did not feel right refusing a future for her fellow servants who would soon be free. She glanced at Tavi. If they ought to refuse it, he would know.

But instead, he settled a hand on Naaman's shoulder, his eyes ablaze with that Light. "The Lord will repay your generosity tenfold, my father. As long as you remain faithful to Him, He will bless whatever you put your hand to, and you will live your days in peace."

To her utter surprise, Naaman's eyes became glassy. "Peace is all I desire. Gold and jewels I need not, so long as I can worship Him."

"And it is because you feel that way that He can trust you with riches as well. Because you will use them for Him, to help others, as you are doing tonight." Tavi dropped his hand and stepped back, his eyes fading from fire to water. He looked over at Atarah and grinned. "You had better help, beloved. There is a lot of packing to do before we must leave."

# CHAPTER SEVENTEEN

Atarah dropped her pack to the ground and indulged in a long stretch of her aching back, breathing in the cool air of evening. Another quiet day of walking, praise be to God. She took one more moment to rub a knot in her back and then turned to the donkey that had been put in her charge. She rubbed the beast's nose, smiling. "Thank you for another hard day of labor, Deborah."

From a few paces away, Tavi breathed what was, for him, a laugh. "You are tenacious in your praise."

Atarah chuckled. The others had teased her mercilessly at first for naming her donkey—and after Israel's famous female judge, at that—and then for praising the creature each day for a job well done. But why not? This little donkey carried far more each day than Atarah did, and she knew how tired *she* was by the time they made camp each night.

Besides, it worked. Deborah had been a shining example of good behavior and even greeted Atarah with loyal affection each morning. Atarah gave her nose another rub and then moved to unload the packs from the donkey's back. The "spoiled grain" was the heaviest, but she had long since grown accustomed to its weight. Then the actual grain they had been eating, the skins of water she would have to refill before they left again in the morning, and the leather pouch with her most precious belongings. A few changes of clothes and the psaltery and lyre Ramina had insisted she take with her.

She settled it on the ground, hobbled Deborah so she could graze without wandering far, and moved to Tavi's side. "May I play tonight, do you think?"

Evenings around the campfire were always a joy. They would reminisce about their homes, about good times in Naaman's house, sing together, dream together of what was to come.

Campfires, however, were not always possible. At least half the nights they had been traveling, Ram's soldiers were too close for them to dare a fire, and certainly not singing. The soldiers moved more slowly than their small band, so Atarah had hoped they would lose them for good within the first week. But their own circuitous path kept bringing them back to where the army was.

Tavi dropped a kiss onto her forehead. "I will go now and scout."

"Alone?"

He cast a glance at their party—down to seven now, soon to be four. Most of Naaman's Hebrew servants had come, not surprisingly, from the lands nearest to the Syrian border. They had already been returned to their families, amid much joyful crying and praises to God. Hence the circuitous route. They had made stops already in villages at the foot of Mount Tabor and throughout the valley of Jezreel, and one near Megiddo. Today they had called a halt to their progress just outside

Dothan and would tomorrow deliver the last three of their companions to be separated from them in villages outside Samaria.

Dafna had no people left to be returned to, nor did one of the shepherds. They had decided to head south with Tavi and Atarah to Ramah and settle near the school.

In reply to her question, Tavi nodded. "I will be fine. Keep everyone quiet and the cook fires small until we know who is around us."

"Of course. Be careful."

"Of course." He winked and then turned to weave his way through the small grove of trees under which they had found shelter.

Atarah pivoted too, ready to tackle the evening tasks. Build a small fire to cook their food, which would blend in with the smoke from the other cook fires from nearby farms. Check over their remaining donkeys to make sure they would be ready for tomorrow's travels. Set up a place for her and Dafna to sleep.

Once in a while they had found a family who agreed to let their group stay in their house or at least within the protection of their fences, but when Ram's group was nearby, they were often too wary to allow any strangers inside. Atarah could not blame them for that. They had given up asking on days when they had spotted the plume of dust from the soldiers' chariots.

Like today.

She hummed as she scouted around for fuel, smiling at Dafna, who was unpacking the pots and utensils and a few precious spices that Naaman had sent with them. Thanks to the cook, each humble dinner had been delicious. She could do the most amazing things with only a few ingredients and a small fire.

Dafna smiled back. "Another new song? I do not recognize that one."

The melodies had practically been tripping over each other in her mind since their journey began. Each day, it seemed, new words, new notes filled her. She grinned at her friend. "This one is all about the joy my tongue experiences each time it tastes your cooking."

Dafna laughed at that, a rich, warm sound that had been sadly missing through the first two weeks of their journey. She had been in Syria for thirty years, since she was no older than Atarah. Naaman's father had been the first to purchase her, and when Naaman set up a home in the city, she had gone with him. His house had been her own for most of her life—leaving it had been like leaving family, and a time of mourning had been required.

Atarah understood that perfectly. She had been with them three years altogether, and she had been grieving the loss too. But the nightly reminiscing had slowly returned Dafna's smiles to her, and then her laughter.

"I imagine there are many good cooks at the school and in Ramah," the older woman said as she pulled out her pack of spices.

"I imagine there are. But none like you. And you must teach me all your secrets eventually." She would have years to do so—she had already agreed to make her home with Atarah and Tavi, taking on the role she was only too happy to accept of Tavi's mother. Their children would be her grandchildren, and Atarah knew her own mother would welcome her as a sister. They did not know exactly where the Lord and Elisha would eventually settle them—perhaps they would stay at the school under Abba's tutelage, perhaps they would eventually be sent somewhere else—but wherever they went, she would go too.

The two other women left in their group, both grinning at the thought of being reunited with their families tomorrow, soon joined them with their own armfuls of sticks for the fire. The remaining two men set about taking care of the animals and otherwise keeping an eye out for any strangers approaching the camp.

They should have felt safe this far into Hebrew territory, where people would not view them as escaping slaves. But they could not, not with Ram always within a day's walk. Any other Syrian commander they would avoid only out of general wisdom, but him… His presence called for more than mere avoidance. It called for complete awareness.

They were all always famished by the end of the day, which made the scents from Dafna's pots all the more tantalizing. Atarah's stomach growled consistently as she washed up at the nearby stream and helped with the meal. So she should have been glad to see Tavi returning a mere hour after he left, just as the food was prepared. Usually they had to leave it to simmer for another hour before he returned.

But an early return meant that he had seen something nearby. Atarah stiffened the moment she spotted him. "So close?"

His face was tight and hard, a careful mask over the worry he would want to hide from them all. "They are a mile northeast of Dothan. Just beyond those farms there, in the grove."

The knots of hunger turned to ones of anxiety. "We should move, then. Find somewhere farther away."

Tavi shook his head though, which surprised her. More than once he had insisted they do just that. "I do not think it necessary tonight. I crept close enough to hear their sentries talking—they plan to attack Dothan in the morning, to seize Elisha. They heard he was there."

Now her stomach dropped all the way to her toes, it seemed. "No."

"They are focused on preparing for their offensive. They will not be worried with who may be hiding elsewhere in the countryside."

"But…" So many thoughts and worries swirled that she could not pick just one question from the beating drums and clanging gongs in her mind. Eventually she settled on, "Elisha. Should we warn him? Sneak into Dothan tonight and get him word?"

Tavi looked half-amused, though it was only a shadow over the mask of his face just now. "Beloved, when has Elisha ever needed the warning of men?"

It was true, but still. It seemed wrong to know that danger was lurking, focused solely upon the prophet, and do nothing to help him.

"Besides, the army is not exactly well hidden. Locals will have spotted them already and warned everyone in the town. If Elisha feels the need to flee, he will do so during the night."

She drew her lip between her teeth.

Tavi sighed. An indulgent sound more than a weary—or harried—one. "Could we at least eat first?"

He was far too good to her. She wrapped her arms around him, gave him a fierce squeeze, and then tugged him toward the small fire. "We will eat, and then the two of us will go. It will give us a chance to see the various paths to the town and know best how to avoid Ram's men tomorrow anyway. We certainly would not want to cross their path when we are about our business in the morning."

"True enough." He made no attempt at trying to dissuade her from coming with him, she noted. She did not doubt for a second that he had such an instinct, but they had all had to do their part to protect the group during the journey, taking turns at scouting and keeping watch during the night. She had accompanied him on small missions several times.

That did not stop Dafna from frowning when Atarah told her their plan as they ladled food into a stack of bowls. "It will be dark before you can get back, and this is unfamiliar territory. What if you get lost?"

Atarah smiled. "A valid fear if it were me alone—but you know Tavi has an admirable sense of direction. Has he once gotten us lost, despite not knowing all the areas we have gone to seeking out our friends' families?"

"No." She granted it with a huff though. "But never before has he ventured away when the soldiers are so nearby. It makes me uneasy."

Which in turn made Atarah second-guess her insistence that they go. She handed Dafna the last empty bowl to fill. "Perhaps you are right. Perhaps it would be wiser to trust that the Lord will warn Elisha and look after our own."

"Elisha?" Dafna paused with her spoon halfway out of the pot, dripping stew. "You said nothing about Elisha!"

Had she not? No, she had only said they would go warn those in Dothan. "Sorry, I must have assumed you knew what I meant. He is rumored to be there. That is why the army has converged upon the town. They mean to take him prisoner. The Lord will surely warn him though."

"He surely will." Dafna finished spooning the stew into the bowl, her face set. "But who is to say that the Lord does not mean for you to be the means by which He informs Elisha? Besides, we owe the prophet everything, for our master's healing. Of course you must go, the moment you finish eating. The rest of us will do your part of the cleanup so you can hurry. I will still feel better if you are back as quickly as possible."

Atarah set the filled bowl beside its fellows and leaned over to give Dafna a sideways hug. "We will be safe, I promise you."

They ate quickly, Tavi eyeing the distance between the sun and the horizon at every bite, lifting his hand more than once to gauge the amount of time they had before it set and increasing his eating speed accordingly.

Atarah matched him and jumped to her feet the moment he did, nodding at Dafna. "Thank you again for cleaning up."

Dafna waved her away. "On with you. Quickly gone and quickly back. We will pray."

"The town is just on the other side of that hill, at the foot of the mountain," Tavi said as they hiked out of their little grove of protective trees.

She took in the landscape and nodded. They had journeyed through this general area on their trip to Samaria half a year ago, so it looked vaguely familiar. They had not ventured this far west before though, off the main trading road between Samaria and Damascus. It was lovely country, with farms and pastures spread out all around them, groves of olive trees, wild myrtle, cypress, and vineyards interrupting the open fields here and there.

But then, all the land they had passed through had been beautiful. Atarah had even gotten her first glimpse of the sea two days ago, when they delivered another of the maids to the fishing village along the Mediterranean coast where her family lived.

Atarah slid her fingers into Tavi's. "By the time we get to Ramah, we'll have seen quite a swath of this land God gave our people."

A corner of his mouth tugged up a few degrees. "All the northern territory, at least. Are you wishing Dafna or Pekah were from Beersheba, so we would have to go to the southern reaches as well and see it all?"

She laughed and stretched her legs a little more to keep up with his ambitious pace. "No, I will be ready to rest in Ramah for a while, I think. But it has been quite a journey. And I will never forget the joy of returning all our friends to their families."

They had witnessed fathers dropping their plows and racing for them, catching up in their arms children they had mourned for dead. Wives spilling their pots into the fire in their exuberance to greet husbands they had never given up on. Brothers and sisters converging on siblings with sobbing tears of praise.

"I will never forget it either." He did not sound happy, though, which made her brows knit as she gazed up at him. He glanced down at her and sighed. "The land is beautiful, yes. And the reunions have been even more so. But have you noticed all the high places? The Asherah poles? The altars to Ba'al? I had hoped to escape such things when we left Syria, but it seems Syria has instead crept into Israel."

Something anyone who had lived among the sons of the prophets knew...intellectually. But seeing it with their own eyes had indeed been different. They had in some ways lived in an oasis at the school, protected from the idolatry by their circle of faithful Hebrews. The teachers and Elisha had all talked in hushed tones about the sins of the land and the consequences certain to come for it, but never had Atarah witnessed anyone actually engaging in such forbidden worship in her homeland.

It had made it easy to think it a sin belonging only to the foreigners who did not know the God Most High. But Tavi was right. It was here, a parasite on the land, threatening all their futures. *That* was why God had allowed the raiders to cross their borders to begin with, *that* was why they had been plagued generation after generation by their neighbors— because they had let their neighbors corrupt what the Lord had set aside as holy.

"What do we do?"

Tavi hopped over a low stone fence that had probably once been part of a sheepfold and reached to help her over too. "What we have always planned on doing. We will learn the ways of the Lord, we will raise our family to follow them, and we will teach them to anyone else who will listen. And, when necessary..." He turned his face back toward Dothan, just visible now, and drew in a deep breath. "When necessary, we warn against the sin, even though it will make us hated. It will not be an easy life if God asks us to do that."

"No." She stepped over a branch and squeezed his hand. "But it is more important to do the right thing than the easy thing. Yahweh Nissi leads us in a better way. I will follow, at your side, no matter how rocky the ground."

Tavi's smile spoke louder than any words could have.

Another fifteen minutes and they were passing the first buildings of Dothan, sidestepping dogs and children being called inside for the night. She had no idea how they would go about finding Elisha but imagined Tavi would soon stop them at a house or a market stall being closed up and ask. Surely anyone who lived here would know where the prophet took his lodgings when he was in the town.

"The well." Tavi nodded at the stone structure in the center of town, which had a crowd of people around it—gossiping, from the looks of it, as much as drawing water.

One man had just finished filling his water skins at least and turned their way. He halted, the setting sun behind him casting him in deep shadows. And then he broke into a run in their direction. "Tavi? Atarah!"

It took her a long moment to recognize the voice she had not heard in years, especially given the tone of it, deeper than she remembered.

Tavi did not seem to have the same problem. He rushed forward. "Abner!" The two met halfway to the well, clapping arms around each other. Atarah followed, though at a more reasonable pace.

Her beloved actually laughed. "I cannot believe it! What are you doing here? So far from Ramah?"

"Me?" His face a wreath of joy, Abner punched Tavi in the shoulder. "What are *you* doing here? We all thought you dead! Both of you." Abner made a quick bow to Atarah, still grinning. "Your parents will be beside themselves with joy."

She could not decide whether to smile or frown. "We are headed home next. But—did Elisha not tell them we had survived?"

"Elisha?" Abner glanced over his shoulder. "He said nothing to them when he came to the school several months ago. But then, he did not stay long, and most of the conversation was about Gehazi."

"Gehazi." Tavi's expression was as careful as she attempted to keep her own. "What about him?"

"Well." Abner motioned Atarah a step closer and pitched his voice low. "It seems that half a year or so ago, some Syrian general came to the prophet, seeking healing from leprosy.

Gehazi was certain Elisha would dismiss him, or perhaps even curse him, but instead he gave him instructions for healing, and the Syrian actually did it. He was healed. They say he offered Elisha more wealth than all of Israel combined could boast, but of course he turned it down."

They knew that part of the story, of course, though clearly no one had shared that they had been among that general's contingent. "But what happened with Gehazi?" Tavi asked.

"He was so furious over the healing that he decided if his master was going to spare the man, then *he* at least would take something from him. He chased after him and made up a story about two sons of the prophets arriving and needing provisions. Then he took the silver—an entire two talents, if you can believe it!—and buried it somewhere near Samaria, then just strolled back into Elisha's house, innocent as you please."

Atarah sucked in a breath.

Abner leaned a little closer to them. "But Elisha *is* the man of God, of course. He knew what he had done and said, 'Where did you go, Gehazi?' and he replied, 'Your servant did not go anywhere' as if he had not been gone half the day, and as if anyone could lie to the prophet! So Elisha replied…" He paused and cleared his throat, even going so far as to change his expression, presumably in an attempt to mimic Elisha, though he did so poor a job of it that she could not be sure. "'Did not my heart go with you when the man turned back from his chariot to meet you? Is it time to receive money and to receive clothing, olive groves and vineyards, sheep and oxen, male and female servants? Therefore the leprosy of Naaman shall cling to you and your descendants forever.'"

Atarah had to clap a hand over her mouth to keep from screeching her alarm. It was not a surprise, not really—she had known there would be consequences to his actions, and Tavi had spoken as much with the Light of the Spirit in his eyes. Still. "He is a leper then?"

Abner's delight with the telling of the tale faded to a more appropriate sorrow. "White as snow, over his entire body. Elisha came to Ramah to tell us the news, knowing how close he and your father had always been. And looking for a new servant." Abner straightened. "I thought he would select one of the teachers, but he said he wanted a young man to train up. One without a family to pull him away from the work, who would welcome the adventure of travel."

"You!" Tavi slapped him on the back, offering a wide smile. "Congratulations, my friend! I can think of no one more deserving of the honor."

Atarah could—but Tavi had been on a different path. And would not, God willing, be long without a family. Although that made her frown at Abner. "Do you mean to tell me you are still unwed?"

His face fell so quickly that she knew to brace herself. "I was betrothed—it was arranged just after the two of you disappeared. Elisheva."

One of her oldest, dearest friends. The one who had always sighed with the most yearning when Abner walked by. "What happened?"

"She fell ill that winter with a fever that stole her from us in a few short days." Abner shook his head, jaw ticking. "I had lost my friend and brother, my betrothed, and my mother followed shortly after. I had no heart to look for any other alliance. I dedicated myself instead to the things of God."

"We are sorry. So sorry." Tavi's hand moved to Abner's shoulder and squeezed.

Abner nodded and then smiled anew. "I cannot complain—here is the friend and brother, returned to me as if from the dead. And I am blessed to be the servant of Elisha himself now. The Lord's hand has not left me."

"Elisha." Atarah widened her eyes. "That is why we have come. There is a Syrian force gathering outside Dothan even now, ready to attack tomorrow and capture him. The king of Syria himself has ordered it."

"He has been a bit frustrated by his raiders being continually foiled," Tavi added. "Can you give him the message? We know the Lord will protect him, but we could not be sure He did not mean to tell him through us, so we hastened here to make sure he knew."

Abner darted a gaze down the road, as if expecting the soldiers to march into sight then and there. "Of course! What of you two? Will you not come with me? I do not often dare to speak for the prophet, but I know he would welcome you at his table."

"Thank you, my friend, but we have others with us we must return to." Tavi stuck out a hand. "We will see you again though."

"You will indeed." Abner clasped his wrist, nodded to Atarah, and turned. "It will be dark soon—you had better hurry back to wherever you are staying, and I to my master."

They could not argue with that. With one last farewell, Atarah and Tavi quickly headed out of the town and toward their companions.

# CHAPTER EIGHTEEN

Atarah rose with the others at first light, rolled her sleeping mat up in silence, and clicked her tongue to get Deborah's attention. The donkey's ears twitched a greeting, but she made no other sound. A strange quiet lay over the land this morning, the sort that even the animals seemed to recognize.

Usually they would have greeted the day and each other with soft words and a quick breakfast. Usually they would have laughed and joked together, and the donkeys would have whinnied their own part of the chorus. Usually a thousand sounds would have made up their daily song.

But today it seemed her very footsteps scarcely made a noise, and Atarah could not make herself want to summon a single sound to her lips. She exchanged glances and nods with her companions, but no one said a word. No one made a move to build a fire. No one needed to consult on whether they would linger and eat or leave.

*Leave. Hurry.* The silent command weighed heavy in the still morning.

Even the more cantankerous of the animals behaved themselves as packs were loaded and pots strapped on, and in remarkably short order they were padding their way out of the grove.

The plan, as discussed last night, was to assume the raiders would move directly south to Dothan, along the road. Their little group, then, would aim themselves southwest on the same track she and Tavi had taken last night and then swing around the city on the western side. They would move as quickly as they could toward Samaria and hopefully avoid the Syrians altogether.

Atarah knew within ten minutes, though, that their plan would not work. Not fully. Because Ram had not ordered his men to come upon the town's main entrance with their whole force. He had apparently spread them wide to surround the unwalled community.

She slanted a look over Deborah's back, toward Tavi. He had halted his own donkey and was staring at the scene before them.

Hundreds, perhaps a thousand Syrian soldiers. Much larger than a typical raiding party, and they stretched out wider as they marched toward the town. There would be no skirting them. They had only two options—to turn back or to head due west and hope to escape their reach, though the mountain behind Dothan would then hinder them drastically. It would mean not making Samaria today.

A small price to pay. Because Atarah knew well they could not simply turn back to their camp. When these raiders were defeated and disbanded, which she knew they would be, they could well flood back over the countryside. She did not fancy being in their way.

*What do we do?* She thought the question in Tavi's direction, still not able to call actual words to her lips. He would be debating the same thing anyway—he did not need her verbalization.

For a long moment, he held perfectly still. And then he spun toward Atarah, fervency in his eyes. One quick scan and he seemed to take in everything near them—the derelict sheepfold he had helped her over last night, the fields, the farmhouse in the distance. Things she had been cataloging too. Things that offered very little by way of protection.

He thrust the reins toward her and pointed at the low stone wall, mouthing the word *"Go."*

What good would that possibly do? And what was *he* meaning to do?

A shout shattered the morning, seeming to come from every direction all at once. The soldiers? She could only assume so, though it was far fiercer a cry than the one Naaman's men had let loose when they flooded over the walls of the school three years before. This was a noise nearly deafening, the sort that could fuel nightmares for decades.

That day at the school, terror had dug claws into her at the shout. This morning it was something entirely different. Something filled her with a rush of strength and broke through the walls of silence.

Her fingers closed around the reins, but she was not about to run away. "What are we doing?"

"Go, Atarah. Get them to safety."

"What safety?" She would not be separated from him, she would *not*. The last time someone had charged her to run and get others to safety, she had ended up a slave.

"Beyond the wall of the sheepfold there was a hidden cellar—did you not see it last night? Look around the branch."

She could only blink at him. She had seen no such thing— but she did not doubt that it was there if he said so. "What of the donkeys?"

"Forget them, let them go. They will run and we can catch them later—the important thing is our lives."

She lunged forward and caught him by the tunic with the hand still holding his reins. "And what of *your* life? Come with us!"

"I cannot."

He looked over his shoulder, and she saw why. A streak of black was headed their way—a horse, its rider letting out a blood-curdling cry as it galloped toward them. *Ram.* It had to be.

"Go!"

She had no choice but to obey—even had she not wanted to, Deborah had apparently decided Tavi's advice was sound and was lurching toward the stones, the only possible cover, paltry as it was.

"Atarah?"

Dafna. Atarah ran to keep up with the donkeys, shouting over her shoulder, "Follow me!" She let go of the reins so the donkeys could jump the low wall and not be hindered, half expecting them to then charge onward without a care for her. In that split second, she bade them a fond farewell—let them take Naaman's money and all their supplies, none of which mattered. They stood a better chance of survival without her and the others, and the Hebrews, conversely, could better hide without the animals.

As soon as she landed from her own leap, her gaze frantically searched the ground. There was the branch. But what had Tavi seen around it?

It took her only a moment to spot it—the edge of stone, the lip of turf that had clearly been cut away and then replaced. "Here!" She motioned the others to drop to the ground, hidden by the sheepfold, and tugged at the tangle of grass and roots.

It lifted away, revealing a cellar some family had likely used for protection from raids before. A few pots and jars sat within, and a crude wooden bench. The space was barely big enough to hold the six of them.

"In, in!" She pushed the others in ahead of her, straining to peer over the stones.

What she saw made her throat close tight. The rider was most definitely Ram, and he would be upon Tavi in moments. Her beloved had unsheathed the sword Naaman had given him, and he gripped his spear in his other hand—thus far on the journey he had used it only as a walking stick or to bring down small game. As she watched, he shifted it to his right hand, took the stance she had watched him master in practice with Seena and Naaman, and sent it flying toward Ram.

Ram pulled up at the last moment, and his horse reared. The spear sank into its shoulder, where Ram had been a moment before, making it lean back even more, wild with pain and fury. Atarah gasped, watching in a combination of horror and gratitude as the animal bucked Ram from its back and darted away.

"What is happening?"

She spun back to the cellar. Her initial estimate had been wrong—only five of them could possibly fit, and besides, she could not just leave Tavi out here alone. She tugged at the sod. "It is Ram. Pray!" With that, she covered the cellar's opening before the horror could give way to any objections.

She dropped to her knees behind the wall. "Lord God of all, our Banner and our Provider. Protect us, I beg You!"

Ram stood with a roar, pulling his sword from its scabbard, his gaze locked on Tavi. "You! I knew the moment I spotted the donkey train that it would be you! What have you stolen from my family now?"

Tavi did not bother answering. He had shifted the sword back to his right hand.

A clatter nearby drew Atarah's gaze to her right. Ram's horse had hobbled over the wall, and the stones must have knocked the spear free. The weapon lay there just beyond her reach, and the horse had come to a halt not far beyond. It was huffing, and blood darkened its coat, but from what she could see it was not too bad a cut.

Good. It was not the beast's fault that its master was their enemy.

She crept to her right just enough to grab the spear and pull it to her side. She had no idea how to actually use the thing, but she felt better at least knowing it was out of Ram's reach.

A clash of metal on metal drew her attention back to the men and brought another frantic prayer to her lips. She did not know what words to use to beseech the Almighty. The sounds she emitted were more notes on the scale than anything Abba would recite at their table. But they were the cries of her heart, desperate for His hand to save.

Tavi and Ram were in full attack, their movements like any number of sparring matches she had watched from the rooftop. But this time the swords were sharp, and the combatants were certainly not friends set on honing each other's skills. This time, murder flashed in Ram's eyes, and she could only imagine what answering spark might have ignited in Tavi's. His back was to her, and she knew, watching him parry and sidestep, that he was keeping it that way deliberately. Keeping himself between Ram and her.

Just as he had done three years ago.

Ram swung down with his sword with a bellow. "I should have killed you that day! I have regretted my failure every day since!"

Tavi sidestepped the heavy blow, made a slash with his own blade, but then jumped back in front of Ram. Usually he would have circled behind. It would have given him a better position for his next thrust. If not for her and the others hiding here, he would have.

Confusion flickered across Ram's face for a moment, chased quickly by smugness. "Either my cousin's darling husband did a terrible job of training you," he said, making another swing, easily parried, "or your sweet little songbird is with those donkeys yonder."

Tavi only grunted and lunged with his blade.

Ram leaped away, though given his wince, his escape was not complete. "Always protecting her, are you not? Well, after I kill you, you can be sure I will finish this where it started, and her corpse will join yours."

Again, Tavi wasted no energy on words. He let out a battle cry of his own, though, as he charged toward Ram, sword raised for another strike.

Atarah was afraid to watch but could not convince herself to look away. Fingers tight around the shaft of the spear, she hummed her prayer to the Lord, its tempo increasing with every thrust met and parried.

Tavi held his own. He would have made Seena and Naaman proud. But he had only been practicing with a blade for three years, and Ram had probably had one in his hand since he was Malak's age. She realized after a few moments that Ram was toying with him—or wanting him to think he was. He wore a snide little smirk that only grew with every move.

Then it happened. Tavi took a risk that she had seen work for him before, but Ram must have been familiar with the move. He jumped away, slashed down with his own sword, and knocked Tavi's weapon from his hands.

"No! Tavi!" Atarah leaped to her feet without quite knowing what she was doing. But in the next second, she had sent the spear spinning through the air. Not aimed at Ram—she knew she could not throw it with enough skill to penetrate his armor. To Tavi.

He caught it, jumped back. Pointed it at Ram.

"Lord my God. Adonai. El Shaddai. Protect Your children!" She could not have said if she screamed it or sang it. If the voices she heard raised with her own were from her friends in the cellar, Tavi, or some host her eyes could not see. She only knew that the air filled with the sounds of voices lifted together, growing until it seemed to fill up the whole sky, as unnatural in its fullness as the silence had been in its stillness.

And then it stopped, and Ram staggered back a step. He raised a hand to his head, shaking it as if dazed. Blinked. His sword sagged to his side.

What was this? Atarah stepped over the wall, cautious but quite suddenly not afraid.

Ram looked at her, but no recognition lit his eyes. Nor did that change when he shifted his gaze to Tavi. "You, farmer. Where are my men?"

Tavi eased back a step. "I beg your pardon, my lord?"

Ram sneered. The same old expression, but gone was the pointed hatred he had always shown them, shown everyone in Naaman's house. He looked upon them as if they were complete strangers. "Put down your hoe and take me to my men, I said!"

His *hoe*? Atarah looked from the spear that Tavi had lowered to his side to her beloved. "What is this?" she whispered.

He shook his head. "I think...I think it is the hand of God."

"Stop muttering in your foreign tongue!" Ram snapped, though they had been speaking as they always did. "Do you know where my men are or not?"

"I do, my lord." Tavi took a step forward. "Come, I will show you."

She grabbed at his sleeve. "Tavi!"

"We will trust in Yahweh Yireh—the Lord has provided." He sounded as incredulous as she felt though and patted her hand in reassurance.

She let him go. Ram had sheathed his blade again and was turning this way and that. He did not seem to see his horse a few feet away though, or the collection of former captives who had climbed out of the cellar. He did not seem to see much of anything.

Tavi stepped more boldly toward him now. "This way, my lord. I will lead you."

"Good. Make it quick. I have an important battle to join."

They took off with matching steps, their strides long and fast. Atarah stood dumbly for a minute, just watching them. Ram's steps were sure. He was not stumbling over every clod and stone and branch. But why had he not seen his horse? Or that it was a spear in Tavi's hand? Or that it was *Tavi*, not some random farmer before him?

"The hand of the Lord indeed," Dafna murmured from Atarah's side. She pressed something into her hand.

Atarah's fingers closed around it without thought, and it took her a long moment to realize it was Deborah's reins.

That was enough to give her a jolt—she spun around and saw that all the donkeys were in hand, and someone had gathered Ram's horse too and was walking it toward them. It had only the slightest hitch in its stride to show the injury it had taken.

She faced forward again. "Come. Let us see what the Lord is doing."

It took them ten minutes at their hurried pace to reach the outskirts of Dothan, where the swarm of soldiers had taken up formation around the city. A knot of them stood at the town's entrance, chattering as if it were just another day, some looking around them as if puzzled. They parted to admit Ram and Tavi into their ranks without so much as a question and did not even blink when Atarah followed behind them.

Tavi marched Ram directly to the head of the crowd. "Here you are, my lord. Your men."

"Good." Ram planted his hands on his hips, surveyed the gathered soldiers, and then spun to face the town.

A figure had appeared in the street. Two figures, both of them familiar. Elisha, standing fearlessly but a few feet away from Ram, and Abner a step behind, his eyes wide.

"What brings you here, friends?" Elisha called out, his voice cheerful and calm.

Ram took a single step forward. "Is this Dothan? We are looking for a man called Elisha."

Elisha laughed. "Dothan? No, no! This is not even the way to Dothan, much less the city. You have made a wrong turn. You need to go south, and a just a little west."

South, slightly west would take them directly to Samaria—a city many times the size of little Dothan, with walls to protect it and the king's army within its gates.

Still chuckling, Elisha repositioned the mantle on his shoulders and stepped forward. "Come, come, follow me. I will bring you to the man whom you seek."

As Elisha strode by him, Ram turned meekly to follow. "You know this Elisha?"

"Does anyone truly know Elisha?" The prophet laughed outright. "But I know him as well as any, I should think. Well enough to point him out to you, surely. Come, it will take us only a few hours to get there."

Ram lifted a hand to his men. "You heard the man. Come! This way."

Not so much as a murmur of dissent rose among the men. They followed like lambs, joking with each other about how they must have gotten lost.

Atarah and the others stepped well out of the way to watch them go by, stopping at Tavi's side. "It is like...like they are blind. And yet they see."

Tavi nodded, looking as dazed as she felt. "As if their eyes can see the road and the figures, but they cannot perceive what they mean."

Abner came up on Tavi's other side. "Do you see them?"

"See who? The Syrians?"

His friend shook his head. "When I told Elisha last night that the Syrians were here for him, he acted as though he did not even hear me. Then this morning, when I arose, I looked out and saw all those men, the horses and chariots, surrounding the city. I woke him and asked him what we should do. But he...Elisha told me not to fear. And then he said..." He blinked, shook his head again.

Atarah leaned closer, as did the others. "He said what?"

"He prayed that God would open my eyes that I might see. And I do. I see them all around. Covering the mountain—horses and chariots of fire, like the one that is said to have swept Elijah into heaven. God's angel army."

Atarah craned her neck all around, hoping and yet fearing that she would catch a glimpse of them. But she saw no flaming warriors. No heavenly chariots.

She remembered the cry of many voices, though, filling up the whole world. "Then what happened? About twenty minutes ago, when the cry went up?" If he could see, then surely he had heard.

A slow, soft smile spread over Abner's face. "My master came outside and faced the army and said, 'Strike this people, I pray, with blindness.' And they became as you saw—their eyes not darkened as one born blind but incapable of understanding what they perceived."

"A miracle, as sure as the one that healed Naaman." Dafna drew in a long breath then let it out. And then shook herself. "Well, what are we standing here for? I, for one, mean to get to Samaria and see what the king will do!"

# CHAPTER NINETEEN

The king seemed just as curious to see what he would do as Dafna had been. Atarah and Tavi and the others managed to hurry around the army and beat it to the walled city, their friends who should have been looking for their families on nearby farms never so much as mentioning the detour. They slipped through the gates just a minute before the army was spotted, just as the hue and cry went out through the streets.

Atarah saw the well she had spotted six months ago, women clustered around it now as then. But they were not singing. They were not scowling at the band of Syrians who had come in peace. They were white with fear over the ones approaching with chariots of war.

"Elisha is at their head!" Tavi shouted into the fray, topping it with a wink for Atarah.

They lingered near the gates until the army drew near, curious as to what Elisha would do. But though they were still, Atarah was keenly aware of the bustle going on around them. People were calling for their children, barring doors, others running by saying they would seek shelter at the king's house. Panic and pandemonium tore the quiet of the streets to ribbons.

Elisha, however, looked as amused as before and not the least bit tired from his ten-mile hike as he passed through the gates. Ram trailed him a step behind, and the rest of the Syrians surged in after them, horses snorting and chariot wheels gleaming in the midday sun.

Atarah followed Tavi's lead, joining Abner just a few steps ahead of the procession. They followed the main thoroughfare through the city, just as Naaman's entourage had done before. Ending, now as then, at the king's house.

This time, however, there was no frowning doorkeeper barring their way. Joram himself stood on the steps, the circlet of gold gleaming on his head and wary wonder gleaming in his eyes.

Elisha came to a halt. The Syrians did as well. "Have them close the gates!"

A murmur rippled, not through the soldiers but through the citizens. Four different runners took off toward the city gates though. Silence stole over the city. Not quite as heavy as the one from the morning but as if the entire congregation had caught its breath.

Five long minutes later, the sounds of clanking gates echoed softly to them. The prophet turned to the king, looking directly at him for a long moment before lifting his face to the sky and raising his arms. "Lord, open the eyes of these men, that they may see."

Wind gusted so unexpectedly that everyone shifted, the soldiers staggering, the chariots swaying backward before the drivers got the horses under control.

Atarah could tell the very second their sight fully returned to them. A thousand sets of eyes widened, curses of shock dripped off of tongues, heads swung this way and that, trying to discern where they were.

She kept her gaze on Ram, who spun in a full circle, clutched at his sword, and then came to a halt, facing them again. His face washed pale, but he did not need to ask where they were. He recognized the city, the king's house, and the king himself as surely as Atarah had. More, he recognized the prophet. His lips trembled, but he said nothing.

Joram pushed forward, elbowing Abner out of his way. "My father! My father, what would you have me do? Shall I kill them?"

Ram averted his face, but he said nothing. He must know as surely as all his men did that they were at Samaria's mercy. Men had gathered from all over the city, swords and spears in hand—the Syrians were surrounded, trapped like a bird in a cage.

Elisha tilted his head, studying Ram instead of the king. "Hmm. No. You shall not kill them. Would you kill those whom you have taken captive with your spear and your bow? No, this is not an honorable thing to do."

Joram looked more confused than disappointed. "What then, my father? Why have you delivered them to me?"

Now Elisha turned to face the king. "Set food and water before them, that they may eat and drink. And then...let them go to their master and report what they have seen."

For a long moment the king stared. First at the prophet. Then at the army. Atarah was not altogether convinced he would obey—he did not, after all, have a reputation for being a king who sought the Lord in all he did. But he must be at least respectful of the man of God. He nodded and called out, "Prepare a feast!"

Atarah and Tavi conferred with their companions and agreed to see the last of them home who would go. They returned from those reunions just as the sun was sinking behind the mountain and found the whole Syrian army seated in a field outside the city, innumerable Samarians pouring them wine and offering them platters of food.

Abner met them with a grin. "Come, you have to be famished. The king's feast is like nothing I have ever seen, and those in Elisha's company are welcome to partake of it too."

They followed him toward a table at the edge of the gathering, where Elisha sat beside the king. And on his other side, Ram. Five places were yet unfilled, and the prophet waved them into them.

Atarah felt small as a mouse as she sat. She had dined with Elisha before, yes, and had been in the presence of two different kings. But never before had she sat with them. Nor—and this was what truly gave her pause—had she ever sat across from Ram.

He looked at her as she sank to a seat. No sneer upon his face. No dark gleam in his eye. He said nothing. Just moved his gaze to Tavi, who lowered himself to sit beside her. Ram's larynx bobbed as he swallowed. "You could have killed me. This morning, when I mistook you for a farmer."

Apparently when the Lord opened their eyes, He had restored to them the memories of what they *should* have seen.

Tavi inclined his head. "I never wanted to kill you. Only to stop you from killing those I love. The Lord did that for me, so there was no need for me to do more."

Ram shook his head. Though a plate of sumptuous-smelling food had been set before him, he did not so much as glance at it. "I do not understand. You had no reason to spare me. Your prophet had no reason to spare any of us. You speak of a God who has the power of heaven and earth—but this is not how I have ever seen power wielded."

Tavi opened his mouth but then just closed it and looked to Elisha.

The prophet chuckled. "Do not look at me, young Tavi. There is no need for me to try to explain what others before me have already put to words so eloquently." Then, oddly enough, he looked directly at Atarah. "Well, my dear?"

She had been reaching for a chalice, thirsty after their long day of walking, but she froze now. "My lord?"

His smile warmed her down to her quaking bones. "Sing this young man his answer."

Sing? In order to convince someone of something? *Her?* She shook her head—this was her imma's part, not hers. Imma would know just the song to sing to break Ram's heart of stone. To make him mourn for all he had done and tried to do. She could make him weep and repent and cry out. But what could Atarah do?

Elisha lifted his brows. "I am no psalmist. But is there not one that begins with a line about the mercies of the Lord?"

The words filled her spirit, her mind, her mouth. "I believe you may be thinking of the eighty-ninth psalm, my lord."

"Well then." He waved a hand.

Something pressed against her side. She looked down to see her psaltery there, in Dafna's hand. Dafna, who grinned and nodded. Atarah took the instrument, then ran her fingers over the familiar planes and strings. She glanced up at Tavi, though she knew well she would find approval in his eyes.

She found more than that—she found one of his rare smiles, looking as settled and at home upon his lips as the people were in the land. It was all the encouragement she needed.

Positioning the instrument on her lap, she let her eyes fall closed and summoned the music to her fingers, to her throat. The familiar words soon filled the night.

"I will sing of the mercies of the LORD forever;
With my mouth will I make known Your faithfulness
    to all generations.
For I have said, 'Mercy shall be built up forever;
Your faithfulness You shall establish in the very heavens.'"

She sang through the verses, lines jumping out at her here and there.

"God is greatly to be feared in the assembly of the saints.... Who is mighty like You, O LORD? Your faithfulness also surrounds You.... The heavens are Yours, the earth also is Yours.... Strong is Your hand, and high is Your right hand. Righteousness and justice are the foundation of Your throne; Mercy and truth go before Your face. Blessed are the people who know the joyful sound!"

She kept singing as the psalm talked about David, about the children of Israel who fell away and forgot the Lord, of His justice in punishing them when it happened. Of how sometimes it would seem as though He turned His face away—but always, always mercy underscored the judgment. Always, always there were the faithful who were preserved to Him. The faithful who yearned to see love for Him return to the land. Who cried out, "How long, Lord? Will You hide Yourself forever?"

It was a long song, but she knew every word, every note, and she sang them to God, offering each one as her own sacrifice to Him. Praying with each word that something in that line, that sentence, that phrase would speak Truth to these enemies feasting with them.

"You prepare a table before me in the presence of my enemies." She did not launch into the twenty-third psalm when she finished the eighty-ninth, but that line filtered into her mind and made her smile as she opened her eyes again. If ever there was a more appropriate lyric for a time, she could not think of it.

Her eyes had been closed for so long that she had to blink a few times to clear them. And then she could scarcely take in what she saw.

Ram was on his knees, weeping at the feet of Elisha.

# EPILOGUE

### Three Months Later

The prophet was coming, and the thrill of what the day would hold made notes of joy burst in Atarah's mind and spill from her lips in a hum. She could scarcely sit still as Imma wove blossoms into her braid, a few ropes of gold tucked in here and there too.

Her mother chuckled and rested a hand on the top of her head. "You are as bad as the twins used to be. Just give me a moment more, my precious one—and then you can dance through the rest of the day and into your bridegroom's arms."

"I cannot help it," Atarah said on a laugh. "I did not think such happiness could be contained in one heart."

"Clearly it cannot, and this is why it is spilling out every which way." Though she clucked her tongue, Imma's eyes sparkled and gleamed. She placed one more flower, sighed in satisfaction, and then clasped Atarah to her chest. "I did not think this day would ever come. Those years when you were lost to us...the tears I cried, the songs I wept. But here you are. The brightest praise."

Atarah clung to her mother. She had done so countless times over the last three months, when the enormity of it all came crashing down again. But she had yet to tire of the free-dom to do so, to reach out and hold and be held.

"Are you ready yet?" Dafna's voice came from the doorway, high with excitement. "I see them coming!"

Imma laughed and pulled away. "Who? The prophet or her bridegroom?"

"Both together, as it happens. And your husband and Abner with them."

Atarah could see that her mother wanted to ask, for the tenth time that morning, if the wedding feast was coming along all right and if Dafna needed any assistance—but she restrained herself, yet again. She had agreed to let the new-comer showcase her skills for the wedding and had focused her own attention upon the music.

Atarah meant to enjoy each part equally. She would feast until she was stuffed, she would dance into the night. And she would sing. She would sing a song to her bridegroom that she had written just for him.

A few minutes later, Abba poked his head into the chamber he usually shared with Imma—the chamber that had been thoroughly overtaken by wedding day finery, to the point that he had declared two hours before that he did not dare to step foot inside and would go await the prophet instead. "He is here! Are we ready?"

Imma turned her to face him. "What do you think?"

Her father gasped, and his eyes gleamed. "My sweet girl—you look just like your mother did on our wedding day. More beautiful than the sun itself."

She smiled and smoothed a hand over the soft linen. Ramina had tucked the fabric into her bags before she left, whispering that it would make the perfect wedding garment. And she had been right. "Thank you, Abba."

"Well then—let the celebration begin!"

There had been no need for the elaborate "coming for the bride" traditions, given that Tavi had built their house adjoining her parents', so they had opted instead to come together in the courtyard of the school at a set time. She made the familiar walk on her father's arm, unable to wipe the smile from her face.

It only grew when she spotted Tavi standing beside Elisha. And saw the smile set upon his lips too.

The words were a blur. The pledges, the promises, the ceremony that made official what she had dreamed of for so long and had thought she would have to dream of for so much longer. But then the shout went up and the feast began and the music started. Atarah's hand was in her husband's, and life was flooding her veins, song spilling out.

Their cups were filled, and Elisha himself stood first. "If I may have the honor of speaking a blessing over the bridal couple."

Atarah, seated at Tavi's side, gripped his hand and smiled up at the man of God.

Abba bowed. "We would all be honored to hear your words, my lord."

Elisha looked over the crowd, then at them. "The Lord always moves in ways difficult for us to understand. He crafts each of us so differently, and He sends us on paths we could never anticipate. When He allowed the Syrian raiders to invade this school, we all thought the two of you had been stolen from us forever—the Lord hid His purposes even from me. But He had His plan, as He always does. A plan to use each of you for great things. Because of your faithfulness, a man received a miracle. Because of your faithfulness, a family embraced the saving God. Because of your faithfulness, the raiders have come no more and we have been blessed with a season of much-needed peace. This will not be the end of trouble between our two nations, but it is a breath of what the Lord promises to those who remain true to Him."

The prophet raised his chalice high. "May the Lord bless you and keep you. May His face shine upon you all your days. May you walk in His ways and teach His truth to the generations to come. And may a song of praise to Him be ever on your lips."

Tavi gripped her hand as everyone cheered and took their first sip of wine. He leaned close. And then he whispered, "Well, my songbird?"

It was not the time she had planned for it. But the Lord always wrote His own song. She closed her eyes, opened her lips, and sang.

# AUTHOR'S NOTE

Years ago I got an inkling of an idea for a story about Naaman's handmaiden, so when I was given the opportunity to write it for the Ordinary Women of the Bible series, I was so excited! And coincidentally (or not!), the weekend after I agreed to the project, my dad (our pastor) preached a sermon on Naaman. Just picture me in the pew taking harried notes.

As I debated the kind of person I wanted to make my main character, this handmaiden mentioned only once, I kept thinking about a conversation I'd just had with my husband about the purpose of praise. Why is it part of our worship? Does God need our praise? Or is the more important part that we offer it, even when it's difficult? Is the point, perhaps, not only for us but for *them*—those who hear and who learn of His goodness through our songs? And so Atarah was born in my mind, a songbird whose praises changed a household.

One thing I loved as I studied this story was realizing the character Naaman must have had. Yes, we see a moment of pride when he first receives Elisha's command to wash in the Jordan. But here is a Syrian general willing to trust a foreign God because of the word of a slave. Here is a master his servants call "my father." Here is a man so beloved by those who serve him that they argue with him for his own good. This is a man worthy of being remembered.

And of course, when I read about the young man who convinced Naaman to obey Elisha, I decided that he and the unnamed handmaiden, the two people who convinced their master to do this thing for which we still know him, must have had a connection.

My speculation that it was Naaman who then told Ben-Hadad about the prophet in Israel who knows what he speaks in his own bedchamber is not explicit in the chronicle in Kings, but it's certainly reasonable! Who else in Ben-Hadad's court would know and trust so fully in the power of Elisha? I thought it would be fun to take this story not just through the healing of Naaman, but through the "rest" of the story as well, and include the miraculous deliverance of the Syrian army into the walled fortress of Samaria that's told to us in 2 Kings 6. The blinding of that army required a bit of creativity on my part—I decided that it made more sense for them still to have some form of vision, otherwise the ten miles from Dothan to Samaria would have been impossible for them all to cover, and I believe we would have seen more panic from them rather than a simple demand that Elisha be delivered into their hands. So just as Elisha's servant's eyes are *spiritually* opened to the angel armies around them, I decided it would make sense to have the Syrians' eyes *spiritually* blinded.

And of course, we don't actually know who took Gehazi's place in Elisha's service, only that he was "a young man." I thought it would be fun to have it be someone we knew.

I hope you've enjoyed reading this tale as much as I enjoyed writing it, and that the next time you lift your voice in praise, you pause to consider the part it could well play in someone's story of faith.

Roseanna M. White

# FACTS BEHIND
## the Fiction

❖

# WHAT WAS NAAMAN'S LEPROSY?

Naaman suffered from a disease that affected his skin, but many Bible experts say it probably wasn't what we associate today with the disease of leprosy—now termed Hansen's disease, which comes from a bacterium called *Mycobacterium leprae*. Physicians today treat leprosy with antileprosy drugs, the only known way to control the disease. Unlike a cold or flu, leprosy doesn't just go away on its own.

One of the most obvious symptoms of Hansen's disease is nerve damage. A person experiences numbness of the affected parts of his or her skin, which often turn white. The person can suffer a burn or a laceration, and without the sensation of pain, they sometimes let the injury go until it becomes so infected that the body part has to be amputated.

Bible writers reported many symptoms of "leprosy," an English word that translates the Hebrew term *sâra'ath*, pronounced (SAW-rah-ETH). But numbness isn't one of them.

A few of the symptoms reported in Leviticus 13:

- "swelling or a rash or discolored skin" (verse 2 NLT).
- "white swelling on the skin, and some hair on the spot has turned white, and there is an open sore in the affected area" (verse 10 NLT).
- "affected area has turned white and the problem appears to be more than skin-deep" (verse 25 NLT).
- "swelling around the reddish white sore anywhere on the man's head" (verse 43 NLT).

These and other reported symptoms could describe patchy eczema, white scale of psoriasis, red swelling of rosacea, and the scaly rash of pityriasis rosea. But most of them are not associated with Hansen's disease.

White patchy skin is an exception. It can be a symptom of Hansen's disease. So some scholars say it's possible that Hansen's disease was one of many skin problems tagged in the Bible as leprosy. But other scholars doubt Hansen's disease existed in Bible times. They argue that there's no solid, supporting evidence from Old Testament times. That includes documents and human skeletal remains. Evidence of leprosy doesn't start to show up until Roman times, about 2,000 years ago. That's the oldest skeletal evidence, discovered in India and Pakistan.

The Bible doesn't describe Naaman's symptoms. It simply says he had "leprosy" (2 Kings 5:3 NLT). But the Bible writer who used the Hebrew version of that word, sâra'ath, was likely familiar with the symptoms reported in Leviticus, a book full of instruction for priests in the tribe of Levi. Priests had the job of diagnosing leprosy—and of declaring a person healed.

Today, an estimated 250,000 people get Hansen's disease every year, according to the Centers for Disease Control and Prevention. It spreads through coughing or contact with fluid from the nose of an infected person. The treatment to eradicate the disease takes a year and a combination of several medications.

## PROPHETS' UNIVERSITY

If a prophet's job was to deliver God's message to the people, then why bother with schools of prophets like those reported in the Bible? What's to learn, some might wonder?

These schools "of the sons of prophets" were led by a senior prophet, such as Samuel, Elijah, or Elisha. All three of these famous Bible prophets had groups of prophets clustered around them, just as Jesus and John the Baptist had disciples who, quite literally, followed them.

ELIJAH IS TAKEN UP INTO THE WHIRLWIND, LEAVING HIS MANTLE BEHIND. BASED ON *ELIJAH'S WHIRLWIND* BY WILLIAM HENRY MARGETSON.

If all a prophet had to do was repeat what God said, even an inexperienced prophet could do that without much training. Amos did. He was a fig farmer who delivered God's messages. But apparently there was sometimes more to prophecy than simply reporting what God said.

For example, Elisha might have taught his students a technique he used for getting into a spirit of openness to hear God's voice. When three kings who were heading into battle asked Elisha if they would win, he said, "Bring me someone who can play the harp" (2 Kings 3:15 NLT). And as the soft music played, "the power of the LORD came upon Elisha." Yes, Elisha said, they would win.

Samuel led the first group of prophets on record. Apparently, part of what they learned was how to worship, since they worshipped together. Newly anointed King Saul met "a band of prophets coming down from the place of worship." They were playing "a harp, a tambourine, a flute, and a lyre" (1 Samuel 10:5 NLT). They were prophesying too.

When the Spirit of God filled Saul, he started prophesying with them. Their response suggests prophecy had become a family business: "Can anyone become a prophet, no matter who his father is?" (1 Samuel 10:12 NLT).

Perhaps student prophets learned the laws of Moses. That was probably the extent of what we now know as scripture available to them. Elisha seemed to attract a big following after Elijah's mysterious departure, swept away in a whirlwind. "One day the group of prophets came to Elisha and told him, 'As you can see, this place where we meet with you is too small. Let's go down to the Jordan River, where there are plenty of logs. There we can build a new place for us to meet'" (2 Kings 6:1–2 NLT).

Schools of prophecy disappeared around a couple of hundred years after Elisha. That is when, in 586 BC, Babylonian invaders from what is now Iraq erased the Israelite nation from the political map. Most Jews who survived the battles were exiled to scattered locations throughout Iraq—apparently to keep the nation from reforming.

Half a millennium later, John the Baptist arrived on the scene. He revived the practice of prophecy and inspired the Jewish people with good news of a coming Messiah.

## WERE PEOPLE OF ARAM ANCESTORS OF SYRIANS?

Although Naaman is recorded as living in the area we now know as Syria, he was a God-worshipping Aramean and the top commander of an army in a small Aramean kingdom based out of Damascus in this region. Arameans had many small kingdoms in cities or made up of tribal coalitions scattered throughout current Syria and neighboring countries. The kingdoms together were known as Aram. Some had a second, distinguishing name. Naaman's home kingdom was sometimes known as Aram-Damascus.

Arameans probably weren't ancestors of today's Syrians, scholars say. Assyrians fought with Arameans to keep trade routes freely open. But eventually the Assyrians overran the Arameans, wiped them out, and assimilated the survivors into Assyrian culture. In fact, Syria takes its name from Assyria. The destruction of the Aramean culture was so complete that there's nothing left to document the Aramean way of life—at least, not that archaeologists have yet uncovered.

Arameans were so adept at blending into other cultures that their language became the most widely spoken throughout the ancient Middle East. By the time of Jesus, most Jews—Jesus among them—spoke Aramaic, the language of the Arameans, in public instead of speaking Hebrew.

Though most Arameans assimilated into other nations, some communities of people today say they descended from the same Aramean ethnic group as Naaman and other Aram kingdoms of Bible times. There's an estimated 15,000 of this group living in Israel alone. Many claim Christianity as their faith.

## LAY OF THE LAND

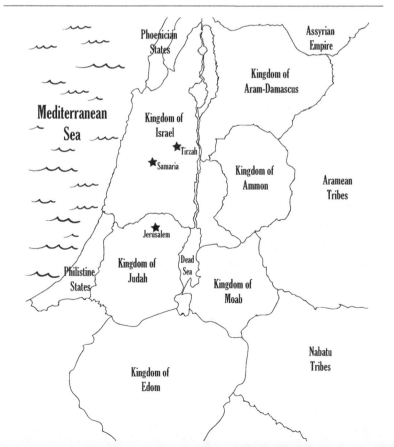

# WHEN AHAB'S FAMILY RULED ISRAEL

Omri ruled six years in Tirzah, capital of the northern Jewish nation of Israel. Then he bought some land farther south, in what became known as the city of Samaria, and he made it his new capital. Omri's son, Ahab, husband of the infamous Queen Jezebel, inherited the throne. The family dynasty lasted three generations, until a chariot corps commander named Jehu assassinated Ahab's son and then declared himself king. Elisha prompted Jehu to do that because Elisha declared Jehu God's choice as the next king (2 Kings 9:6–7.) By contrast, David didn't kill Saul after Samuel anointed him king. David waited for Saul to die. Jehu was less patient. He wiped out the entire royal family and displayed their heads by the city gate. The prophet Hosea said that God punished Jehu for that by making him subject to the Assyrians.

Jehu's image of him kissing the ground before the Assyrian ruler, Shalmaneser III, after bringing him gifts is chiseled into stone. The picture is part of an Assyrian document known as the Black Obelisk, created in about 840 BC. A century later, in about 722 BC, Assyria overran Israel and wiped it off the world map. Only the southern Jewish nation of Judah survived. A century and a half after that, in 586 BC, Babylonian invaders wiped Judah off the map too.

# WHERE DID THE SAMARITANS GO?

Assyrian invaders from what is now Iraq leveled the cities of Elisha's homeland in about 722 BC, probably killing or exiling many of Elisha's descendants. Suddenly, the northern Jewish nation of Israel was gone, including cities in the region of Samaria, where Elisha lived.

Assyrian records and the Bible agree: after the war, Assyrians sent pioneers to resettle the Jewish land. Some Israelites who had evaded Assyrians and stayed in Israel married settlers. Those blended families living in the region of Samaria became known as Samaritans. Or perhaps the land became known as Samaria, named after the Samaritans—scholars are not certain.

SAMARITAN HIGH PRIEST AT TURN OF THE 1900s. BASED ON A PHOTO BY MATSON. SOURCE: LIBRARY OF CONGRESS.

Samaritans say "Samaria" comes from a word describing them: *samerim*, "keeper" of the laws of Moses. They say they prefer to be called Israelites—the only true Israelites. In fact, Samaritans revere the first five books in the Bible, which contain the laws of Moses. But they skip everything else in the Hebrew Bible—no psalms, prophets, or proverbs.

They also reject Jerusalem as the holy city of God. They worship at Mount Gerizim in the Samaritan hills, as the first-generation Israelites did. Moses commanded it, and Joshua fulfilled the command (Deuteronomy 11:29; Joshua 8:33).

Samaritans still sacrifice animals at Passover. That's something Jews no longer do, because the Bible says they can sacrifice animals only at the place God selects (Deuteronomy 12:11), and Jews say He selected

Jerusalem. There hasn't been a Jewish temple there since Romans tore down the last one in AD 70, while crushing a Jewish rebellion. Instead, now crowning the temple hilltop is a 1,400-year-old Muslim shrine, called Dome of the Rock, built there after Arab invaders captured the Holy Land.

Samaritans say they consider themselves the true Israelites. But Jews came to describe them as heretics worshipping a warped version of God and reading a Bible edited to diminish the role of Jerusalem and to ignore the prophets who came after Moses and spoke for God.

By the time of Jesus, animosity between Jews and Samaritans was similar to the bad blood between Israelis and Palestinians in recent decades. Samaritan-Jewish conflict is what made Jesus's parable of the Good Samaritan so captivating—a Samaritan helping a Jew.

In the centuries that followed the ministry of Jesus, Jews and Samaritans slaughtered each other in riots and battles. Romans sometimes reestablished the peace by killing those they considered troublemakers. In the long haul, Samaritans came out the losers. They were nearly wiped out, reduced to as few as one hundred left.

Today, nearly 1,000 Samaritans live mainly in two communities in their native land. Some still live at Mount Gerizim, in the West Bank land claimed by Palestinians. Others live on the outskirts of Tel Aviv, in Israel.

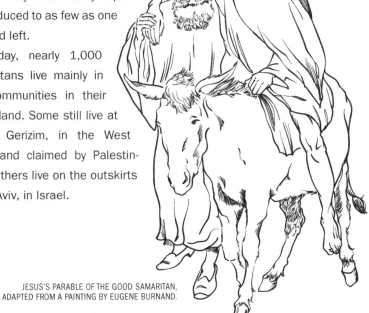

JESUS'S PARABLE OF THE GOOD SAMARITAN,
ADAPTED FROM A PAINTING BY EUGENE BURNAND.

### Fiction Author
# ROSEANNA M. WHITE

**Roseanna M. White** is a bestselling, Christy Award winning author who has long claimed that words are the air she breathes. When not writing fiction, she's homeschooling her two kids, editing, designing book covers, and pretending her house will clean itself. Roseanna is the author of a slew of historical novels that span several continents and thousands of years. Spies and war and mayhem always seem to find their way into her books...to offset her real life, which is blessedly ordinary.

### Nonfiction Author
# STEPHEN M. MILLER

**Stephen M. Miller** is an award-winning, bestselling Christian author of easy-reading books about the Bible and Christianity. His books have sold over 1.9 million copies and include *The Complete Guide to the Bible, Who's Who and Where's Where in the Bible,* and *How to Get Into the Bible.*

Miller lives in the suburbs of Kansas City with his wife, Linda, a registered nurse. They have two married children who live nearby.

*Read on for a sneak peek of another exciting story in the Ordinary Women of the Bible series!*

# DAUGHTER OF LIGHT: CHARILENE'S STORY

## by Melanie Dobson

Darkness shrouded the alleyway as Charilene rushed home. Late once again.

A lantern flickered on the street ahead, and in the distance, she could see lights on two ships anchored in the harbor waiting to either unload their goods or sail back out at daybreak to deliver their new wares across the Mediterranean. If it wasn't so late, she'd stop along the shore for a few extra moments, just to listen for the Spirit whispering in the wind.

More than anything she wanted to hear God speak like her sisters did.

Her family was used to her being late for meals, but tonight they would worry. A traveling missionary named Paul and several of his companions had stayed in her family's villa for several weeks now. She was supposed to be there hours ago, helping her sisters host a banquet before their guests left for Jerusalem.

But she lost track of the hours as she helped her friend Renata prepare a dinner meal of barley groats and beans. Renata's husband, a captain of a merchant ship, was out at sea, so Charilene had stayed after the meal to show their children a new toy attached to a string, which her sister Iris had made.

On one side of the small disc, etched in the clay, was an antelope eating grass. On the other side the animal was leaping into the air. Charilene had spun the string over and over, and the children were mesmerized as they watched the antelope jump whenever the disc circled between her hands.

Darkness had come upon them as they played, and when the room grew black, Charilene had leapt to her feet like the antelope. Her sister Eustacia would be furious that she had missed the dinner preparations. Eustacia liked things to be done with precision, while Charilene's world seemed to ebb and flow, changing like the tide.

Now alone in the darkness, Charilene lifted the hem of her tunic and hurried toward the market street. During his time here in Caesarea, Paul had encouraged their entire church community. She didn't want to miss a single story about his travels across Asia Minor and Greece.

Abba used to travel like their guests, but now that Imma was gone, he spent much of his time at home. While Charilene enjoyed hearing the stories, she'd been born in Caesarea nineteen years ago and wanted nothing more than to spend her life in this seaside town with her father and sisters.

But things were changing here and across Israel, the animosity growing for those who had decided to follow

Christ. Word was spreading that the current Caesar, a young man named Nero, hated those who followed The Way. This animosity from Rome seemed to be trickling across the entire empire.

Abba had begun to talk about leaving again, and she dreaded the thought.

Firelight blazed across the wall to her right, streaming down another alley, and she stopped. The pounding of sandals drummed up the path, and her heart hammered like leather against stone.

Romans, she guessed, legionaries patrolling the perimeter of the city. They guarded the wall so an attacking enemy didn't try to scale it or a citizen didn't transport untaxed goods to the other side.

She didn't want them to think she was attempting to leave town.

Slipping back into the concave of a doorway, Charilene pressed into the shadows as the sound echoed around her, the drum of feet shaking the stoop. The men, she prayed, would march past or turn the opposite direction.

A lantern light swept across her face, blinding her. If only she could sink deeper into the shadows.

"Stop!" The commander's voice was a low rumble, like thunder before a storm. And while her heart raced, their march grew still.

She lifted her hand to block the light, trying to see the man in front of her.

"Why are you out tonight?" he demanded.

It was Decimus, the centurion in Caesarea. He reported directly to Governor Felix, a man suspicious about the growing community of disciples in this town. But as long as their community continued to pay taxes to Caesar and didn't cause a riot in the streets, Governor Felix allowed the people here to worship whatever god they pleased.

Decimus was more indignant about The Way. He'd visited their community last week with one of his soldiers, and when Abba asked if he'd like to join their meal, Decimus responded with a slap across her dear father's face.

"I was visiting a friend," she said, praying quietly for strength.

He seemed to study her face in the light, cornering her in this place. "I know you."

"I'm on my way home."

The centurion turned back to legionaries who accompanied him. "Leave us."

The soldiers slipped away like grains of sand into the sea. And she was left alone with this man who towered over her.

He lowered the light, placing it on the ground next to his wooden cudgel. "You are the daughter of the one they call Evangelist."

Fear taunted her, making her voice tremble. "My abba is Philip."

He stepped closer. "What did you say?"

"My father," she repeated, trying desperately to be strong. "His name is Philip."

"Your father is spreading lies in this city."

She shook her head. "Abba is offering freedom through Christ."

"No one can break free from Caesar."

"I must return home." She tried to slip around him, but he wouldn't let her step back into the street.

"My men will stop this spread of lies."

She shrank against the cold stone again and hated herself for it. This man who stood before her may be as tall as a gladiator, his shoulders broad, but he was still only a man. The heavens contained an army of angels armed with weapons that no human could withstand.

His hand came down over her mouth, and she muttered beneath it, begging God to send His army. Begging Him to deliver her from this evil.

"I will show you the truth," he said.

Another hand went to her shoulder, the force bruising her skin. She'd heard of Roman legionaries doing the unthinkable to women, but not here in Caesarea.

She never should have been walking in the dark.

Her world started to turn gray, his hands groping her tunic. Instead of an army, perhaps God would send darkness. She could fall completely into the shadows.

The black of a stormy night, that's all she saw now, the stones rocking under her feet. It wouldn't be long now.

She started to slip away when she heard another sound. A woman's voice calling her name.

"Lena?"

Decimus turned quickly, and in a sweeping motion, her older sister pushed her way around the centurion and grabbed Lena's wrist, yanking her back out into the street. An angel in human form.

"Does the governor know that you are accosting our women?" Eustacia demanded, lifting her oil lamp to meet his glare.

He spit on her face. "I don't answer to you."

Her sister slowly lifted her hand and wiped the spit off with the back of it. "But you must answer to Adonai."

"I don't do the bidding of any god except Caesar."

Eustacia tugged on her wrist again. "My sister is coming with me."

Even though she and Eustacia were often at odds, Lena wanted to hug her in that moment. Eustacia feared God alone, never any man.

Decimus reached for the wooden stick and held it out to block them. "Is that Jewish man still in your home?"

"Which man do you speak of?" Eustacia asked.

"All of your guests are stirring up trouble in Caesarea."

Eustacia nudged Lena toward the other passage, even as she continued to speak. "You will be relieved to know that they have left the city."

"I am not convinced of that."

"Our community meets on the first day of the week," Eustacia said. "You and your men are welcome to return. I will be speaking next—"

Decimus lowered the cudgel. "I will not listen to a woman."

"We are going home now," Eustacia replied, giving him no choice but to listen.

He transferred the club to his right hand. "It won't be your home for long."

"For as long as God allows it," Eustacia said.

Decimus only meant to threaten them. Scare followers of The Way from helping those in this city who needed food and a friend.

Or scare Charilene into succumbing to his whims.

She shivered again, wishing she could wash away the press of his hand.

Governor Felix had not allowed his men to persecute the followers of The Way, not like those who lived in Jerusalem. The governor was curious, it seemed. Amused, even, by their belief in a resurrected Jewish man. But if his curiosity waned— or Decimus decided to take action without the approval of Rome—her family would be his first target.

After Decimus turned to follow his soldiers in the alley, Eustacia tugged her along the opposite direction as if she were Lena's mother. But this time she didn't complain. Her sister had scared Decimus away.

"Thank you," Lena said.

"That man's pride is going to be his demise."

"When did Paul and the others leave?" she asked.

"This afternoon, while you were out—" Eustacia stopped when they reached the well-lit market square with several merchants closing their booths for tonight. "Where were you exactly?"

"With Renata."

Eustacia shook her head. "You cannot keep wandering these streets alone."

"Did Abba go with Paul?"

Her sister sighed. "He did."

Lena glanced back toward the alley as if Decimus and his men might still be watching them. She didn't like her father to leave Caesarea, but this time she was glad that Abba had gone.

# A NOTE FROM THE EDITORS

We hope you enjoyed *The Prophet's Songbird: Atarah's Story*, published by Guideposts. For over 75 years, Guideposts, a nonprofit organization, has been driven by a vision of a world filled with hope. We aspire to be the voice of a trusted friend, a friend who makes you feel more hopeful and connected.

By making a purchase from Guideposts, you join our community in touching millions of lives, inspiring them to believe that all things are possible through faith, hope, and prayer. Your continued support allows us to provide uplifting resources to those in need. Whether through our communities, websites, apps, or publications, we inspire our audiences, bring them together, and comfort, uplift, entertain, and guide them. Visit us at guideposts. org to learn more.

We would love to hear from you. Write us at Guideposts, P.O. Box 5815, Harlan, Iowa 51593 or call us at (800) 932-2145. Did you love *The Prophet's Songbird: Atarah's Story?* Leave a review for this product on guideposts.org/shop. Your feedback helps others in our community find relevant products.

*Find inspiration, find faith, find Guideposts.*

Shop our best sellers and favorites at
**guideposts.org/shop**
Or scan the QR code to go directly to our Shop

# Find more inspiring stories in these best-loved Guideposts fiction series!

## Mysteries of Lancaster County

Follow the Classen sisters as they unravel clues and uncover hidden secrets in Mysteries of Lancaster County. As you get to know these women and their friends, you'll see how God brings each of them together for a fresh start in life.

## Secrets of Wayfarers Inn

Retired schoolteachers find themselves owners of an old warehouse-turned-inn that is filled with hidden passages, buried secrets, and stunning surprises that will set them on a course to puzzling mysteries from the Underground Railroad.

## Tearoom Mysteries Series

Mix one stately Victorian home, a charming lakeside town in Maine, and two adventurous cousins with a passion for tea and hospitality. Add a large scoop of intriguing mystery, and sprinkle generously with faith, family, and friends, and you have the recipe for *Tearoom Mysteries*.

## Ordinary Women of the Bible

Richly imagined stories—based on facts from the Bible—have all the plot twists and suspense of a great mystery, while bringing you fascinating insights on what it was like to be a woman living in the ancient world.

# To learn more about these books, visit Guideposts.org/Shop

Made in United States
Orlando, FL
26 September 2024

52000778R10153